The Wolf

Is Not Native

to the

South of France

The Wolf
Is Not Native
to the
South of France

WILLIAM WISER

Harcourt Brace Jovanovich

New York and London

Printed in the United States of America

A portion of this novel was published in
McCall's in slightly different form.

Library of Congress Cataloging in Publication Data

Wiser, William.
    The wolf is not native to the south of France.

    I. Title.
PZ4.W82Wo [PS3573.187]   813'.5'4   77–84396
ISBN 0–15–198023–3

First edition

B C D E

for

Paco and Anne Karin

The Wolf

Is Not Native

to the

South of France

One

At the end of the third month of living alone Paul saw (or thought he saw) a small girl playing in the garden below his balcony. There was no one there, but he saw her all the same.

"Christine?"

Why did he call her that? As soon as he spoke aloud she went into shadow and there was only a patch of artichokes where she had been.

Paul had the habit of visions. He once told Duff about this aberration, his home movies of the mind, and Duff warned him off books, especially fiction, and told him to go easy on the late-night TV. But that was a year ago, and the last book Paul read was—well, he forgot. There was no television at the Mas Mazarin.

Two days later she appeared again. The scenario was the same; he was slightly lightheaded at the end of the day, he had a premonition that something unexpected (but not unwelcome) was about to take place. His first impulse was to pour a drink, light a cigarette, but instead he drifted into a pleasant lethargy; he made no move other than to glance toward the sea, check for clouds, go with the drift. The atmosphere changed subtly, as if he had one ear in a seashell and a finger in the other. Traffic on the lower Corniche came to a standstill: the sound of automobiles diminished, then ceased. (All his private movies were silent films—no sound effects, never voices.) There was a sudden flash of color against the green: a bird, he told himself that first time; a butterfly now.

He resisted the instinct to speak her name. Christine, he remembered, was the name they had chosen for a daughter if a girl, instead of Jean-Paul, had been born. This was not a vision to be tampered with. Paul could, without strain, elaborate on an image until he had a panorama, a tapestry— in full color, if that was the mood. The daydreams were deliberate, but this was different: a little girl had come to him out of the blue, lingered, and then was gone.

Paul had been separated from his wife since the end of summer, but he had convinced himself they would be back together again before Christmas. Meanwhile he went into tedious decline. A thin Cincinnatian to begin with, he had in the last three months lost weight. Despite a native optimism, a positive outlook and a background of faith (his widowed mother was a Christian Scientist), his sleep was ragged and plagued with dreams. He had edged up from one pack of cigarettes to two, and down (for economy's sake) from Benson & Hedges to Gauloises Bleues. The years in France— twelve, the new year would be his thirteenth—had helped develop a taste for wine; he was an American still, and liked a cocktail before dinner, or stronger stuff: vodka, cognac, *eau de vie*, when he could get them. Lately he drank more than he should, but less than he wanted.

When he did sleep he dreamed of his wife and son, but his dreams were different from the casual visions of midday; in dreams he could see Sylvie and J-P as if through plate glass, their voices filtered through a poor telephone connection, distorted by static—or twenty thousand leagues under the sea. Neither of them would look at him, ever, as they spoke together in complicated French using the subjunctive he had never learned, full of argot he could not follow. Though they were in the fishbowl, he was the one drowning on the other side of the glass. His most frantic, even desperate, gestures failed to catch their attention. He sometimes woke shouting aloud, "Listen!"—and as soon as he got his breath, and knew where he was, hoped the elderly sisters downstairs had not heard. He was fascinated by the way his hand trembled lighting a cigarette before dawn. Most mornings his pillow was wet, whether from tears or perspiration he did not know.

The first part of the day passed tolerably enough: he worked mornings writing a column for *Grimwald's Overseas Guide*, a monthly newsletter for tourists published in Monte Carlo. As a correspondent for the *Guide* his territory was that lush region between Toulon and the Italian border, the Riviera and environs. When he had to, Paul ventured forth to inspect the food and lodgings at noteworthy restaurants and hotels; his visits were anonymous, in the tradition of Baedeker and Michelin. Writing for the tourist trade was no burden, no strain: you could always, in France, find something to say about even the most meager *prix fixe* meal. Hotels were harder (and sleeping in them, for an insomniac, impossible)—the new ones were neo-Provençal, imitation Hilton or replica Holiday Inn; the old ones were just old. Paul, however, had the gift of his visions; he was capable of spinning something out of nothing.

He wrote under no other pressure than a mid-month deadline and the occasional ghostly echo of Grimwald's warning, "Keep it upbeat." Upbeat was Grimwald's word, along with, "The *Guide* is a publication with a smile," though he never said it with one. Anyway, the editing was done by Miss Bishop, and Miss Bishop could always put a smile in Paul's copy when the prose turned sour. I am the comparison-shopper of the open road, Paul told himself—it was hack-work, but harmless. Grimwald, Miss Bishop, could do as they liked with the text; Paul never bothered to read the printed version of his peripatetic travelogue. The column appeared under the heading: "The Phantom Inspector—What He Sees & What He Says," one of Grimwald's lesser inspirations, but an easy title to live up to.

In addition to being the Phantom Inspector, Paul was sometimes "Rowland Thompson" for *Sunspots*, a travel quarterly published in London, or "René de Cygne," a free-lance contributor to brochures distributed to members of the Club des Voyageurs, headquarters in Geneva. His earnings from secondary sources, under assumed names, were sporadic and mostly trivial, but he hesitated to inform Grimwald he was moonlighting outside the *Guide*. Grimwald, who saw the world through square-cut bifocals and whose favorite American was Benjamin Franklin, might consider Paul's divided loyalty technically unethical or accuse him of being a double agent.

One clear cold day in December (but not too cold to work on the balcony, warmed by a generous sun, wearing a sweater Sylvie's mother had knitted) Paul removed his Oli-vetti from its felt-lined casket, asking himself, "Who am I today?" He had just yesterday finished and delivered his column for the *Guide*, and there was an empty morning ahead of him.

He could not be René, because he needed Sylvie's help with any text in French, so he must be Rowland, and would have to remember to write "lift" instead of "elevator." He resisted the temptation to change the typewriter ribbon, switched off a beginning dawdling daydream and forced himself to roll a blank sheet of paper into the typewriter. There is nothing, thought he, as blank as a blank sheet of paper.

This was one of those mornings—end of one job, beginning of another—when Paul was hard put to wait until noon for the first drink of the day. He promised himself another cup of espresso, as a pick-me-up, but no alcohol till the stroke of twelve (his watch was unreliable, he would count the strokes) from the belltower in the village. He braced his feet solidly against the tile and began to type: "Nowhere in the world would you find—" What?

If he had the espresso now it might pump a surge of adrenalin into his brain. Better now than too near the apéritif hour: the opposing drinks would cancel each other out. No, he would wait till the stroke of ten, and at least one page of clean copy, before having another coffee.

"Nowhere in the world would you find a paradise to compare with—" What?

Maybe he would rewrite the piece on that seafood restaurant in Theoule for the British audience—substitute "prawns" for "shrimps"—was that plagiarism? He would just be stealing from himself. Recycling, was a better term.

He had pulled back from his typewriter, debating the moral issue of an outright rewrite, half watching for the little girl, Christine, to appear (though she never came out in the cold light of morning, she was a sundown creature) when one of the Mazarin sisters called to him from the garden. The two old ladies, the propriétaires, wore threadbare towels across their shoulders, as shawls, and identical straw hats—Paul could not tell Mademoiselle Béatrice from Mademoiselle Bérénice.

There was no telephone at the Mas Mazarin, and Sylvie had called the postmistress at Roquebrune to tell the mail carrier to deliver a message through the sisters: Monsieur Swanson was to please retelephone Madame at his earliest convenience. Paul dropped a *merci* like a blessing from the balcony.

But his hand shook, so he lighted a life-sustaining cigarette.

"Sylvie?"

"*Oui?*"

"It's Paul."

"*Je sais.*"

Speak English then, if you know. (Another bad connection, like those voices in his dreams.)

"How's J-P?"

"*Il est bien.*"

"What did you plan for Christmas?"

"*Il voudrait un arbre de Noël.*"

"What?"

A woman outside the booth glanced unhappily at her wristwatch, waiting to use the *cabine automatique.*

"He wants a Christmas tree."

At least she had come around to English, down to earth; they were maneuvering on his terrain. The advantage of language was hers: she spoke fluent French, Italian, German and English; Paul's French was adequate, but not as good as her English. (When he discovered the French were not only articulate, but conversational autocrats, he managed to acquire enough French to express the basics, then resigned himself to listening.) Sylvie's deliberate switch to French was as if she had gone back to the formal *vous* after ten years of calling him *tu.*

Her cool superior tone unnerved him; hearing her voice—in any language—undermined his grip on himself. His legs went weak, he could not think what to say next. There was a time when she depended on him, when her voice wavered wondering what *he* was thinking. Paul tried to summon up a note of authority with an undertone of nonchalance.

"Let's get him one, then."

He barely got out of the booth before the impatient woman with the wristwatch squeezed in. She gave him a look of exquisite disgust as she fanned at his cigarette smoke with the Alpes Maritimes directory.

Two

They had driven so long in silence, somebody would have to speak soon.

"Trees are sky high this year," said Sylvie, finally.

The pines beside the road grew instantly higher; their topmost boughs touched the lower part of the sky. (He had never been able to tell Sylvie about the visions: she would call them hallucinations, meaning D.T.'s.) He wondered if J-P saw the trees shoot "sky high"—his son's English was so literal. But the boy only squirmed uncomfortably as another silence fell.

"Yesterday," Sylvie went on, "I saw a tree in Grasse that cost forty francs."

"Yes?" Paul tried to make his voice sound astonished—or at least interested—but his thoughts were elsewhere. He once did an ad for Amazing Growth illustrated by a money tree with bank notes of every denomination—francs, lira, pounds, dollars—sprouting generously from the branches. Now, beyond the hood of the car a spirit tree glittered—just out of reach—decorated with ten-franc notes instead of colored lights and tinsel.

A small animal darted across the road well ahead of the car, and J-P shouted, "*J'ai vu un lapin!*"

"We speak English when Papa is here."

Papa is here, thought Paul happily: "I saw it too."

"It wasn't a rabbit," said Sylvie, "it was a rat."

"I saw a rabbit," said J-P, and Paul wanted to back up his son, but he was no longer certain what he saw—visionaries make unreliable witnesses.

With Sylvie's statement the pines shrank to life size again and the money tree disappeared. Across St. Cassien Lake they could see the scarred hillsides where the mimosa burned last summer—a warning, a blight, a Biblical plague. According to *Nice-Matin* it was a grudge fire deliberately set by some Snopes out to revenge a lost lawsuit, but Paul suspected the fire was caused by the usual careless tourist flicking a lighted cigarette out of his car. Still, this part of the Var was primitive redneck territory, where an *Anges d'Enfer* motorcycle gang roamed the back country roads and the populace believed a flying saucer had landed at Montauroux. Newspaper stories out of the Var ran to: Drunk Freezes to Death in Abandoned Cabanon, Hunter & Dog Double Suicide Behind Bird Blind, Grandmother Raped by Tax Commissioner.

Maybe there was a rabbit *and* a rat—too late, however, to offer this theory. Paul believed compromise was the key to most dilemmas; he thought he might make a first-rate Foreign Minister at Large, if the world would accept a daydreamer in that post. He did not know what Sylvie considered the key to most dilemmas, certainly not compromise. Still, she was trying hard—he wondered if she thought he was trying hard enough. He would have to try harder. It was Sylvie, he kept reminding himself, who had made the first move. She had even consented to let him drive—but she sat in the back seat, J-P at her side. Paul sat alone in the front, like a chauffeur.

The region they traveled was the rugged province just west of the Alpes Maritimes where Sylvie and Paul lived (in opposite corners, as he sometimes thought of it, like boxers). They had crossed the Siagne, the dividing line between the two provinces—still known as a trout stream in the upper reaches, but a sluggish cesspool by the time it reached the sea. Beside Paul on the empty seat was a newly purchased ax from Monoprix, its vicious head wrapped in brown paper. (When Paul bought the ax he had tested its weight, lumberjack fashion, before the perplexed salesgirl—for he could be playful, even childish, when his mood was bouyant, as it was then and had been ever since Sylvie called.) He wanted to think of himself as a pioneer woodsman, and might have worked up a pioneer portrait of himself versus the forest primeval—but he could not extend the image to Sylvie as his pioneer wife, or to J-P (who called Indians peaux-rouges) as his pioneer son. They passed a junkyard garage flanked by rusted gas pumps, they passed a roadside garbage pit behind a sign that said DEFENSE DE JETER DES ORDURES. The forest, he had to admit, was hardly primeval either.

Over the hill and through the woods to grandmother's house we go. They were traveling the woods first—the hills were beyond. And grandmother's house was in Geneva, as far as J-P was concerned. (He had never seen his American grandmother in Cincinnati.) How odd to have a son who was truly French. Almost as strange was to have a wife who was Swiss. He felt the strangeness now, but usually he only thought of it when he was away from them. When they were together his French son and Swiss wife seemed the only wife and son he could reasonably have.

To the north were mounds of snow-capped stone above the oak forests and green pine of the *arrière pays*, but they would not drive beyond the wooded foothills. The Alpes Maritimes in the distance led to the Basses-Alpes, to the Hautes-Alpes, to the Swiss Alps and to grandmother's house after all.

A billboard alongside the road said TERRAIN À VENDRE with a telephone number to call. Sylvie asked aloud, "I wonder how much it is worth, a square meter?"

"Even the wilderness is for sale," said Paul.

"What's wilderness?"

"Wilderness," said Sylvie, "is where nobody lives."

"Where nobody lives—yet."

The Var, he knew, was the next to go. Real estate that touched the shore was no longer real: the coast so over-built new homesteaders were heading inland. Now vineyards and olive groves and forests of cork oak were bulldozed under to make way for summer villas and *supermarchés*.

"Except the animals," said J-P.

"Right," said Paul. "The Peaceable Kingdom."

"What's that?"

"Where the lion shall lie down with the lamb." Paul tried to catch Sylvie's eye in the rear-view mirror, but he could see only one side of her face, and on that side the corner of her mouth was turned down.

"Is there hunters in the Peaceable Kingdom?"

"Are there hunters," said Sylvie.

"No hunters," said Paul. "Just us."

"There are hunters everywhere," said Sylvie, who did not like to see a myth go too far. (She had made certain J-P knew Père Noël was really Maman and Papa, but two years after she told him this he was still writing letters to Père Noël.)

"No hunters where we're going," said Paul. "I know a place."

"Except only Christmas tree hunters," said J-P.

"Right."

Paul did not know anyplace free of hunters in this season, this side of the Siagne, but he could imagine a place the hunters had overlooked. He saw the place in his inside eye, a forgotten corner of the Peaceable Kingdom, the last empty place before the world moves in.

However, when they got to evergreen country, and Paul slowed beside a stretch of woods that had to be the place, he noticed (too late to speed up again) the grim evidence of empty paper casings from expended shotgun shells. Nearby were the charred remains of what could only have been a hunter's fire.

He managed to park the Opel directly over the cartridges and burned ground. If Sylvie noticed, she said nothing. It was a relief not to be told I told you so.

The car door on J-P's side flew open, and the child leaped out ready to embrace the wilderness or whatever lay ahead. Sylvie seemed flushed. With pleasure? Paul asked himself. Well, something. She was a graceful creature; she had a sense of herself, a stylish way of getting into a car or getting out of one. Paul swung the ax—as light now as a broom handle —to his shoulder. He hoped he looked something like the picture he saw of himself. A Pilgrim father, thought he, is what this family needs. No, that is not what this family needs. What this family needs—but he could not think what.

Once again Paul reminded himself that it was Sylvie who had called him. The three Swansons were setting out together under an unbelievably brilliant December sun. After all, it was not a divorce—only a trial separation.

Three

Paul bore a quaint stippled scar above his left hip, an indelible codicil to their marriage vows, a covenant signed in blood. The wound was a result of a kitchen drama seven years ago; no vital organs had been pierced, and he told the intern who had stitched him that he stumbled and fell with a pair of scissors in his hand. He was x-rayed, sewn up, bandaged and given an antitetanus shot at Les Broussailles, in Cannes—the hospital where J-P had been born four months before.

This unexpected episode was the first of a series of small disasters that nagged them ever since. Before that had been the heady Belgian honeymoon, then the long sunny year in Cannes—almost a second honeymoon except for occasional morning sickness as Sylvie's belly swelled. He was working for Duff then, making more money than he could keep track of (but Sylvie could), settling into the tranquil southern European scene. Those were the champagne days, Cannes was the great good place before the baby came—Paul tried not to go there any more.

J-P had been a remarkably unhappy infant from the start. He cried nonstop, and seemed to sleep only long enough to store up energy for the next marathon crying bout. What was the source of his misery? Paul discovered the term "colic" in Dr. Spock, but their pediatrician in Cannes knew of no equivalent in French. Dr. Freiné gave Paul to understand European babies were never like this, and Sylvie hinted that Paul must have transferred his damaged American colic genes to their son.

Sylvie had a plentiful supply of milk (her Swiss-brand Nestlé, Paul once called it—she was not amused) and the baby would suck hungrily enough, but then he would screw up his little red face, stare wildly into the void and lustily regurgitate everything he had taken in. The milk shot out in one long powerful jet as if from a distended wineskin, cruelly squeezed. Pyloric stenosis, according to Spock; yes, agreed Freiné, *stenose du pylore.* More common in boy babies than girls; no great cause for concern as long as the baby gained weight, which he did. He did not always vomit his feeding, but when he did Paul was usually hovering in the vicinity with sponge or diaper in hand and got the stream of vomit across his shirtfront.

At first Sylvie was perplexed, then hurt, by the failure to calm or feed her baby. The dark circles under her eyes were like bruises; she staggered through the day on nerves and coffee, she slept only when the frantic baby slept. In frustration she stalked Paul through the small apartment accusing him of everything and nothing. They engaged in deadly verbal combat: accusation followed by recrimination, sobs, shrieks—all on an ascending scale that inevitably aroused J-P to new heights of screaming protest. It was summer: Paul pulled the shutters tight to spare the neighbors; Sylvie threw them open again to gasp for air.

Paul had the daily escape of work; for Sylvie there was no exit. But Paul, too, was fretful if not desperate: he sought advice from the salesmen at Amazing Growth, from waiters, even from the elevator operator (who was from Normandy, and suggested adding a jigger of Calvados to the baby's milk). At last he went to Duff (married but childless), who said, "Get a nurse, for Christsake."

Of course. But Sylvie would not hear of it. She allowed the concierge to clean for her a few hours every week, and Paul did the shopping; but the expense of a nurse was out of the question—she did not want another woman in the house, she would not tolerate the interference. If extra help was what she needed, she could always ask her mother to come down. Paul could not hide his horror. His vision was of Madame Chaix flying down from Geneva on a broom. It was all they needed to make purgatory complete: his indomitable mother-in-law onstage, a fourth at family torture. Sylvie resented the expression on his face.

"What expression?"

"Every time I mention Maman."

"Did I say anything?"

"It's the way you looked."

Which ended in tears and cold towels.

When things did get worse Sylvie changed pediatricians. Dr. Secours had never heard of colic either, but he prescribed théralène to help the baby sleep, and recommended feeding by formula. Sylvie was not ready to give up breast-feeding, and she was suspicious of tranquilizers, for babies, but meanwhile she recalled an appointment she had made weeks ago (while she was still pregnant) with a homeopath in St. Raphael. Dr. Grandjacquot was so popular new patients were obliged to seek a first appointment at least eighteen weeks in advance. Sylvie admitted she could no longer remember why she had made the appointment—whatever malady she had, had long since disappeared—but so many failings had developed in the interval she had sufficient medical inventory to make a consultation worthwhile. The appointment loomed so large in her mind it seemed to dominate her every thought: she referred to Dr. Grandjacquot daily, with infinite enthusiasm and absolute trust—as if she knew him already, and had consulted him before—until even Paul began to believe the homeopath would save them all. The day was circled in red on the Crédit Commercial calendar;

Paul would take the day off, drive them to St. Raphael that afternoon. He had a portrait of the good doctor in his collection of images (and Sylvie must have had the same portrait in mind): the venerable features of a Chinese sage, the simple manner of a saint.

Two days before the appointment a telegram came. Dr. Grandjacquot was ill.

Paul came home that evening to find Sylvie sitting transfixed at the kitchen table, three disemboweled fish laid out before her on sheets of *Nice-Matin*. He assumed his wife's unnatural calm was due to the fact that the baby was, for once, mercifully asleep. Sylvie was like an automaton; she worked queerly, stuffing twigs of fennel into the stomach of a *daurade* she had slit open with a pair of scissors. She did not respond to Paul's greeting, nor did she look up at him, but went on stuffing the fish as if her life depended upon it. When he moved close and bent to kiss her she stabbed him with the scissors.

Four

It was a lyric moment. Sylvie stepped out ahead of him, slim hipped, with the determined pace of a mountain hiker. The path was springy with pine needles and Paul walked several inches above the earth. Her tailored skirt and nylons, out here in the woods—perfect. Time and circumstance meant nothing: Paul had fallen in love with his wife.

He studied her figure closely, stared at her back and waist and buttocks. Suddenly, for an instant, he saw her standing naked against the rust-colored leaves, posed perfectly against the autumn backdrop. He had memorized her body after all these years and he knew her flesh as well as his own. He wanted to touch her, encircle her with his arms, now, and claim her for all time. Since he was a thoroughly captured man, he must capture her too. Fearing neither her temper nor her tears, he reached out—but at that same moment she was instantly clothed again, his elusive unfathomable wife, walking ahead of him into the woods, as distant and unattainable as a nymph in a painting in a museum. Paul bit his lip until it bled.

J-P hovered at his mother's side—to protect her, it seemed: he was, after all, her escort. A thin, quiet, introspective child, he was almost cocky now—he might have carried a hunting knife in that holster, instead of sugar. (He wore a leather holster strapped to his belt with a supply of sugar cubes in case of malaise, and a medallion around his neck that said: *"Je suis diabétique."*)

Sylvie carried her sensible-looking leather purse on a shoulder strap, like a dispatch case; in the purse would be forty francs, at least, in case the evergreen they chose might turn out to be *à vendre*. She was always prepared for the worst. ("Why not?" she once told Paul, "The worst is what always happens.") There was surely an emergency hypodermic in her purse, too, against insulin shock. And an I.D. card with the notice, in three languages, that she was allergic to penicillin. She had long insisted that Paul keep a tag in his billfold that stated his blood type, in case of a highway accident that required a transfusion. There was a snakebite kit in the glove compartment.

In truth, Paul loved her as much for her practical purse as her delicate ankles and low-pitched voice. He had loved her in that time of despair when she turned to him for support, and he loved her now in her new-found confidence and pride. (Hard to believe she had ever been helpless, his wife, who was now so sure of herself as to work crossword puzzles with a pen.) She delighted him in unexpected ways: the spectacles she wore—granny style, halfway down her nose—were comic, true, but it charmed him to see her wearing them when she checked the Bourse columns in *Nice-Matin* for price fluctuations in Swiss gold francs. He knew her every gesture, her look, her smell, her flesh—but who was she?

Sylvie must have sensed he was staring at her back, for she turned. (He stared at the back of her head as if looking through a washing-machine porthole, trying to see the thoughts that tumbled around inside.) When their eyes met, Sylvie was the first to lower hers, and she almost stumbled.

J-P had quit the path to indicate, hopefully, an awkward-looking evergreen. He wanted to be the one to have discovered the tree they would take home.

"A little lop-sided, don't you think?" said Sylvie.

J-P did not know the word lop-sided, and while Sylvie explained, Paul saw his own lop-sided tree, the money tree, in his mind's eye. The shade from that tree had long darkened their lives. It was top heavy with foreign currency (and Swiss gold francs) and could never be cut down and chopped into kindling, though possibly dying of blight.

As for a Christmas tree, even J-P must have known Sylvie would make the final decision. Paul was proud of this ability of hers to choose swiftly and well, that certainty of mind she displayed at a fruit stall or cheese counter: Sylvie invariably moved in on the single melon that was perfectly ripe, or scooped up a camembert that was exactly à *point*. Paul was content to be woodsman with the ax. He would be called upon to cut the tree that Sylvie decided was the most beautiful in the forests of the Var—and there were possible rewards for being a pioneer in the south of France he could only anticipate for now.

Meanwhile, he was in no hurry for the hunt to end. Once the tree was selected, cut and carried off, the outing with his family would be over. He quickly checked the sun to make certain it was not going down before its accustomed hour.

The path turned back on itself, a U-turn between the saplings, and Paul took a shortcut through the undergrowth to catch up with Sylvie. They walked together for a time, Paul only a pace behind her, keeping in military cadence to her step so as not to tread on her ankles—until Sylvie moved self-consciously ahead to inspect a cluster of evergreens. The situation was as delicately awkward as going out on a first adolescent date, and he tried to think how not to push himself too eagerly upon her and yet not hang back too far. He quickened his pace, but kept his distance.

Civilized was the word for Sylvie—he was captivated by her civilized outward show, with the prospect of that lovely croissant of hair unwound (for him) across a pillow, the tailored skirt across a chair, her soft and pliant body pressed to his. I am sniffing after this woman, he told himself, for in the brief moment he had walked beside her, her perfume had washed over him and made his knees go weak—but another part of him stiffened (this is degrading, thought he), and he tried to walk in a way that would not reveal himself aroused.

It was not the perfume he had given her last Christmas, and he loved her for not wearing a scent that did not suit her —a negative way of love, like loving her colorless lipstick for its very absence of color (it made her lips seem cold, and he wanted to kiss them to life) or loving the suede jacket she wore simply because it was hers. In his eyes she was a European beauty, a treasure that did not fluctuate in value on the Bourse: he loved her for her priceless, civilized European self.

Now, as they plunged off the path to a part of the forest cut off from the sun, he lost the faint trace of Sylvie's perfume—a kind of spoor he found himself following; here it smelled damply of mold and mushroom. He preferred the pine-scented air stirring the dead leaves of the oaks, and he lifted his head into the slight, chill breeze that came down from the canyon cliffs. He could not see the river, but he stared out across the valley the Siagne traversed, knowing the headwaters originated in those barren mountains. There, thought he, at the rim of that frosting of snow, is the beginning of the last empty place in the world.

He was looking far beyond the surrounding tangle of greenery and dead leaves into a bank of clouds above the last visible mountain when he thought he heard another sound through the voices of Sylvie and J-P. A low, persistent, rumbling sound. He could not be sure where it came from, and at first he thought it might be thunder, the growing threat of a storm that echoed against the wall of cliffs. No one else seemed to notice. It grew louder, an ominous trembling of the earth that only Paul's private seismograph recorded. Sylvie and J-P chattered with excitement as they converged on a single tree: the perfect tree, Paul knew at once, but his instinct—as foolish as his love—was to shout, "Not that one!"

The beast emerged abruptly out of a black thicket of thorns. Only Sylvie cried out, and her scream was quickly strangled in the paralysis that had fallen upon them all: they froze in panic at the incredible sight of a wild boar galloping in their direction. The animal charged directly toward Sylvie, and it was she who would be mangled first by those ugly tusks that pierced the monster's snout. It was as if Paul were watching from a distance, standing apart, mesmerized by one of his visions, and thought was his only function, for he could not move: the ax was welded to his shoulder. In those few seconds of terror, more thoughts flashed through his brain than he would have believed possible: could he grab J-P and perch him on the limb of the nearest tree? If he shouted "Go back!" to the shaggy brute, should it be in English or French?

Then, for no apparent reason, the boar slid to an awkward halt. It, too, seemed paralyzed, struck dumb in its confusion: who was the hunter here, who the hunted? For a brief eternity Paul stared into the creature's pig eyes set so far back on so huge a muzzle the animal seemed all head and no body. The head appeared so evil in aspect the boar might have been a gargoyle, graven in flesh instead of stone. Paul could imagine the ax swinging downward to split the head in one swift guillotine stroke—but the instrument did not leave his shoulder.

The boar snorted, turned suddenly and scrambled back in the direction from which it had come. There was an explosion of broken brambles where the creature disappeared, and even as Paul did, this time, snatch J-P into his arms—still clinging to the useless ax, Sylvie stumbling over a barrier of mossy rock in retreat—they could hear the boar crashing its way through the dead leaves.

"*Un sanglier! C'était un sanglier!*" shouted J-P, screaming the beast's name, as frightened and happy as he had ever been.

Sylvie, trembling, fed J-P two cubes of sugar from the holster, to prevent a malaise.

Sylvie drove. Paul was not certain what his place in the back seat meant: he had J-P beside him, but the smell of the beast—a smell of fear and loathing, instead of Sylvie's delicate perfume—still lingered in the car.

"*J'ai fait pi-pi.*" J-P confessed he had wet his pants, and Paul said lightly, "I almost did myself," but Sylvie said nothing. Paul noticed her hand still trembled when she touched the gearshift. The ax handle protruded ridiculously between Paul's knees, the unused blade still swathed in its original wrapping paper. They had come away without a tree. No one was hurt, but Paul knew some unspoken harm had come to them back there in the woods.

Sylvie would have felt J-P's pants to see how wet they were, but Paul took his hand from the ax handle to stretch one arm like a wing across his son's bony shoulders. The child responded like any small animal in an uncertain world: he nestled close.

Paul wished he might see Sylvie's lips under the colorless lipstick, but all he saw was the upswept crescent of hair, and her hands, the knuckles white, clinging to the steering wheel as if to a life ring.

J-P spoke French now. The pitch of his excitement had diminished, but his talk was of the *sanglier*—its size, how close to them it had come—and, too, his exuberance was partly due to the sugar cubes he had swallowed minutes before. Paul remembered something the butcher in Ys had told him about boars: only the female will attack, and then only to protect her young—but they had not lingered there to test the theory. J-P did not express his disappointment that there was no tree, finally, to take home. If there had been a tree he would be speaking English, thought Paul. His son was apt to express his delight in English, his fears in French.

But Sylvie no longer bothered to remind J-P to speak English because Papa was there. English, the language of diplomacy, was finished for the day. It reminded Paul of fights with Sylvie, arguments that began in English but soon became bilingual when Sylvie switched to French and left him hanging there, struggling for verb forms in frustrated anger, searching for equivalents of goddamn.

But there was no argument in any language, and that was the trouble. Paul sat with J-P in the back seat, but almost more alone than when he had sat alone in the front. He brooded on this. He nursed the fear of the beast and the feeling more damage had been done to them in ten frightening seconds in the woods than all of the years before. He tried to conjure up happier thoughts of Sylvie and himself, mental remembrances of birth and birthdays, the Belgian honeymoon, days and nights together in the stone villa at Ys—but whatever visions he hoped to nourish were invariably erased by the image of a medieval monster breaking through the thorny undergrowth.

All the while Paul was searching the road ahead for the turnoff that led to Ys. That would be the literal turning point in the day's adventure: if Sylvie turned off, it meant Paul was going back to the villa with them, perhaps for supper, and a chance to see J-P off to bed. (The last time he had stayed for supper he was stacking dishes when he heard Sylvie, through the bathroom door, painfully explaining to J-P: "No, Papa does not sleep here any more. He is going back to Roquebrune tonight.") But when they came to the road to Ys, Sylvie did not turn off.

"Is this the way home?" asked J-P—for they were still on

the Draguignan highway, heading for Grasse.

"We're taking Papa to his bus."

J-P made no comment, and sat back tucking himself once more into his father's wing. Paul had not really expected his luck to turn dramatically, and he was disappointed only in the way of a tiercé player who knew his chances were ten thousand to one. But he was annoyed with himself for his lack of status: Sylvie, who once depended on him, now decided which direction he would take.

They were already on the outskirts of Grasse, but were blocked by the long funeral file of mourners walking behind a plumed *pompes funèbres* coach headed for the narrow cemetery just outside of town. Sylvie's finger drummed impatiently against the steering wheel as the car inched through the choked traffic along the Jeu de Ballon—they lurched forward as soon as the funeral procession turned off.

Just before they came to the bus terminal, they passed the Monoprix where Paul had bought the ax (I should ask for my money back, was his thought), and outside the supermarket a *paysan* stood patiently beside a stack of Christmas trees, their rope-bound limbs drawn up like folded umbrellas.

"They look like they're in straitjackets," said Paul, who really thought they looked like corpses, an image touched off by the black display of the *pompes funèbres*. "How about if I pick up one for J-P?"

Paul could feel J-P stiffen and hold his breath while Maman went deeply into her shell of contemplation, taking several leaden seconds to reply: "All right. I'll try to park. Do you have money?"

Paul quickly checked his billfold to find he had barely more than bus fare home. That damned ax. Money does not grow on the money tree (his wife would have told him) and he was obliged to murmer: "Ah, maybe not enough."

Sylvie found a temporary spot behind a line of taxis; she pulled over to the curb and took fifty francs out of her purse. Paul accepted the money with his eyes averted. He scrambled over J-P's lap and was out of the car instantly; he made straight for the tallest of the trees and quickly asked: "*Combien?*"

"*Quatre mille.*" The man stepped forward briskly and spun the tree a couple of presentation turns. Like most Frenchmen in the Midi, he still spoke in old francs. Paul automatically canceled the last two zeros: forty francs. Forty francs (he made another instant calculation) was nearly nine dollars. He hesitated—since the money was not his, but only for a second—then handed over the fifty-franc note and received a dog-eared, disintegrating ten-franc bill in return. The tree was his. Even trussed-up as it was, he knew when its limbs were spread it would be a duplicate of the tree they had seen in the woods. Paul hoisted it to his shoulder; the evergreen's prickly stickiness was almost a caress to his cheek, but he carried the day's bounty to the car as much in defeat as in triumph.

J-P's face bloomed beaming at the car window. Even Sylvie's colorless lipstick covered a thin smile, for Paul's knitted watch cap had caught in a branch of the tree and now hovered like a black halo several inches above his head. It was worth looking foolish, playing Chaplin, to bring Sylvie to life again with a ghostly smile.

"Forty francs," Paul said to her, before she could ask. "Same price as that tree you were talking about."

"It's dear," she said (her word for expensive), as she awkwardly folded the shabby ten-franc note back into her purse.

"Maman says you will come back with us to arrange it,"

said J-P. English was the medium of communication once again.

"Sure." Paul did not want to sound indifferent, but not too eager either—he was still on shaky ground. "We can use the same two slats we used last year." Sylvie never threw anything away. "And that old tire from the Opel as a tree stand. Remember?"

J-P remembered.

When the tree was jammed into the back seat with its topmost branches poked through an open window, Paul won another sly victory. He would have to sit up front with Sylvie. She backed the car out and made a careful U-turn at the bus terminal. As they drove along the old Route Napoleon bound for Ys, Paul felt Sylvie's body near, was reconciled to her scent—but he was also aware of the leather purse pressed between them on the seat.

Five

It was a small stone villa on two thousand square meters of terraced olive grove, surrounded by a hedge of cypresses, a hillock of pine and oak behind the house. Sylvie carried the key to the house in her purse. The property belonged to her, if it belonged to anybody: the land had passed through the hands of Greeks, Phoenicians, Romans, Gauls, Italians— to the Mazarin family, finally, for a century or more—now to a Swiss housewife and her American husband. Paul had restored the interior of the house, replastered, replaced the sills and rotted beams, put in copper plumbing and a septic tank, then scrabbled in the soil to make a lawn, to make a garden. He could smell the garden in the dark.

The house was in Sylvie's name, but it was not yet hers. She had paid down a quarter of the total selling price to the Mazarin sisters (those same elderly *demoiselles* Paul rented from in Roquebrune) and would pay a monthly rental for as long as the original owners lived. The sisters had never married, they had no heirs: selling the house by *viager* would give them a small income, an old-age pension to supplement their Sécurité Sociale, for life.

(Paul once proposed an article on the *viager* system of real estate, but Grimwald said it was too downbeat for American readers; he wrote it anyway, and sold it to a real-estate trade journal in London under his British pseudonym, Rowland Thompson.)

As for the property in Ys, Paul was doggedly opposed to the purchase. "It's immoral, waiting around for two old ladies to die."

There was even a third sister, Madame Roustan in Ys, widowed, with no claim to the property other than *droit de passage*, the legal right to trespass along an established path through the oaks and pines to her rabbit hutches on the other side of the hill—she exercised this privilege at weird hours, passing phantomlike between the cypresses with a burlap of greens on her back, across the driveway, and sometimes (J-P reported) lifting her skirts in the woods behind the house to piss among the pines.

"We're not waiting for them to die," said Sylvie.

"It's indecent."

"It's just a business transaction." Sylvie saw ingenious possibilities for restoring the rundown property, and the restoration would make the house a valuable investment. "In five years the place will be worth four times what we're paying."

"How do we know what we're paying?" Only death would close the sale.

"In France it's just another way to buy a house." Sylvie had her granny glasses on and was scribbling sums on the back of an envelope. "Remember, the installments are fixed when the contract is signed. Inflation hurts them, not us."

"I don't want to hurt anybody."

"I'm talking about inflation."

"And I don't want to drink champagne at somebody's funeral."

"You don't have to drink champagne," she said, annoyed. "It's only normal to be relieved when you don't have to make payments any more, but—"

"It's like making book on somebody's death."

Sylvie did not know what "making book" meant, but she said: "They'll die when they die, like anybody else. Even if they live to be a hundred, we'll still come out ahead."

Ahead, a head. Paul remembered the grim term *"deux têtes"* in the real-estate ad, meaning two heads would have to roll, instead of one—which brought on the image of a guillotine, the Mazarin sisters kneeling under the blade, Paul and Sylvie wearing appropriate black hoods.

Sylvie was determined to buy the place. Paul refused to sign a *viager* contract, and the sisters would sell no other way. While Paul went on looking for another house, Sylvie retired into her shell still scribbling sums on the backs of envelopes.

They had married in France under the ancient Code Civil (devised by Napoleon, that conjugal malcontent), which in most respects reduced a wife to the status of minor dependent: she could not open a bank account without her husband's signature or take a job without his permission. Paul agreed the marriage laws were blatantly unfair, so they signed a contractual agreement before marriage that would allow Sylvie to maintain financial independence. It occurred to Paul that love and death and money were so inextricably entwined (and matters too serious to be left to the parties concerned) they had to be regulated and documented by embassies and notaries and at city hall. Though they were married in Paris by the mayor of the Eleventh Arrondissement, Paul suspected the actual wedding had taken place in the notary's office in Geneva, where he and Sylvie signed the prenuptial contract called *séparation de biens*. As far as Paul could follow, with the scrappy French he knew at the time, the *séparation* meant whatever belonged to the husband belonged to the husband, whatever belonged to the wife belonged to the wife. But later the troubling notion nagged at him that he might have signed away more than just a share in Sylvie's linen chest and bank account, but had, in some peculiar European way, relinquished the husband's traditional role.

Two old men in wing collars and shoes that buttoned above their ankles had waited in the anteroom with them, then joined them for the conference with the notary. Paul was more intrigued by the elderly gentlemen than the dry legal proceedings under a cut-glass chandelier, in an office with stained-glass windows and chairs as hard as pews. He watched the old fellows lean forward, their chins on their canes, listening with apparent rapture to the notary's ecclesiastical chant. The notary was reading in a monotone the contractual clauses of a document that ran to more pages than Paul dared estimate. At one point the notary paused, fixed Paul with a glacial stare, then turned to Sylvie to ask if her future spouse understood the declaration thus far and was aware that both parties to the agreement were formally bound to the separation of their worldly goods until the dissolution of their marriage by death or divorce. Sylvie translated. Paul nodded and Sylvie said, "*Oui.*"

Then Sylvie was called upon to read aloud her list of personal possessions: the declaration ran to four pages, including her Limoges dinnerware, a ten-speed Peugeot bicycle, as well as shares in Nestlé her father left her. Paul was hard put to come up with anything besides his typewriter and a wristwatch that lost ten minutes every twenty-four hours. Sylvie reminded him of his suitcases. Any insurance? asked the notary. Ah, yes, a ten-thousand dollar G.I. policy (lapsed when he got out of the Army, but Paul claimed it anyway). Camera? No, but this reminded Sylvie she had forgotten to include her Leica on the list. Paul could not help smiling, and he suddenly wanted to kiss Sylvie's ear, or light a cigarette with a dollar bill—anything to brighten the scene, break through the sober fiscal mood—but Sylvie's expression was set in stone, he had never seen her as serious.

Serious, too, were the gentlemen in wing collars and buttoned shoes; one had wiped his lips with a handkerchief when Sylvie read aloud her list of possessions, both had bowed their heads when Paul read his. The notary spread the portentous documents across his desk for Paul to sign, then Sylvie—six copies at least—and the two old men signed after them. Were they relatives, he later asked Sylvie, or friends of the family? Sylvie had never seen them before; they were professional witnesses.

She had married him when all he had was a typewriter, two suitcases and a watch that ran slow. If money made so little difference in the beginning, why should it loom so large now? But Sylvie had become accustomed to a salary that grew with Amazing Growth, a salary commensurate with the superlatives Paul employed (he wrote the advertising copy himself). When that job sank out of sight—the company went under, no fault of his—he went to work for *Grimwald's Guide*. He was convinced, in spite of all, he could still support a family of three on $150 per thousand words of travelogue for *Grimwald's Overseas Guide* and an occasional free-lance essay on the side. However, Sylvie had married the Amazing Growth adman, a creature of infinite promise, and ended up with the bankrupt Phantom Inspector.

The money for the down payment on the house had come from Madame Chaix.

"Does that satisfy your moral objections?" asked Sylvie.

"No."

But there was no further discussion of the *viager* issue (no more than the tepid protest he made when Madame Chaix paid for the Opel Kadett), and Paul was perversely relieved when the deal was done. Sylvie signed the transfer deeds at the office of the notary in Ys and came back to Cannes with a leather binder full of papers and an antique key as heavy as a paperweight.

"Does this make you my landlady?" asked Paul.

"Don't be silly."

Her mood was exuberant, and for the moment she could accept any comment, any sarcasm. She kissed him as a way of saying he was still master of the house.

The fact is, he wanted to tell her, we're tuned into the universe on different frequencies: you're on the narrow European band, while I come in several megacycles lower on American short wave.

Yet, her enthusiasm was contagious, and Paul was caught up in her aura of good will. They had a late supper of fondue with an excellent bottle of Chambertin. How loving she had been that night. For a little piece of eternity, in bed, he forgot about the deaths of old ladies and the weight of a brass key as he lost himself in his wife.

Six

The boy was pitifully thin in the bathtub, his little stub of a penis growing hard under the warm flood. Paul turned off the water. Sylvie had warned him to fill the tub just below the level of J-P's navel: water was taxed heavily if they used more than the half a cubic meter daily allotment. The bathroom had the same chrome and ceramic-tile look of a modern American installation, but it was French and chilly. The butane gas heater was on. There was a draft: Paul had opened the window onto the garden because the leaky heater was dangerous in a closed room. The rest of the house was heated by accumulator radiators, a Gallic mystery: the radiators were cumbersome devices theoretically storing up heat during the night, on cheaper electrical current; they gave off gasps of smelly heat in the morning, but were stone cold by noon and seemed to refrigerate instead of warm for the remainder of the day. (There was, fortunately, a wood-burning fireplace in the living room faced with baker's tiles, and Paul had scattered an assortment of coil heaters in the bedrooms and hall after the laconic electrician in Ys suggested the radiators would operate more effectively if the rooms were heated first—one of those amusing but exasperating French theories about how things work.) The house was damp from late fall through winter and a sponge in the spring rains. Paul studied the black patterns just above the tile border on the garden-side wall of the bathroom: he would scrub away the offensive mold come summer and repaint in drier weather, even though the same tainted traces would grow back by winter. He was oppressed by what he saw in the dark Rorschachs on the wall; he turned from those evil mushrooms back to his son.

There were moments when life came within a hair of being tolerable—like now. A shadow lifted, Paul was at ease. He pictured a magnetic field of paternal love over and around the slim figure in the bath, warming J-P in a way the gassy butane heater never could. As soon as J-P stepped out dripping onto the shag rug, Paul enveloped him in the smothering tent of a double-size bath towel, as if to make a package of him and smuggle him across some border. Now where did that thought come from? Paul asked himself. That was the trouble with letting movies of the mind run on. His son was not a piece of contraband to be sneaked through customs into another country.

He felt the boy's ribs under the yellow terrycloth, the clavicle like a fragile wishbone—how vulnerable he was, yet how substantial too. Paul vigorously massaged the thin straight dew-speckled back and purposely lingered over the two sharp protruberances—were they really vestigal wings? were we all angels in another life?—but when his hand swept down the ridges of the spine to that taillike stub end of the coccyx, he realized we could have been devils as well.

J-P pulled on his outgrown pajama top, turned wrong way around, the *cheval au galop* galloping backwards: the color print turned outside in. Paul would have left it as it was, but Sylvie would be annoyed; so he took it off and reversed the galloping horse before J-P could get his arms through the sleeves.

While J-P did his urine test Paul sat on the knitted pink toilet-seat cover (a gift from Sylvie's mother) and watched. J-P thrust his miniature male organ into a test tube and filled the tube halfway; then, with an eyedropper, he measured out one drop onto an acetone capsule.

Through the bath steam J-P called to his mother: "*Pas d'acetone.*"

"*Bon,*" replied Sylvie from the kitchen.

No acetone. Good.

Into another tube: five drops of urine, ten of water, a Clinitest tablet into the melange. After the liquid foamed, J-P began counting to fifteen—"*Un, deux, trois—*" and then the mixture turned orange, finally olive drab. J-P compared the color to a color chart on the bathroom wall and sang out to his mother: "*Un croix seulement.*"

Only one cross. Not even Christ, reflected Paul, had to carry more than one. He recalled the day J-P came home from the pediatrician's office, bursting with the news: "*Je suis diabétique!*" in a delirium of happy excitement to have discovered he had become so special a person. Sylvie stood in the doorway nodding yes, her eyelashes damp, it was all true, while J-P chattered merrily on: Maman had even bought a chicken so they could practice injecting the carcass (a new word in English he pronounced car-case) until everybody knew how. Eventually, when he was a little older, J-P could give himself the insulin shots as long as someone else pinched up a place for the needle.

Paul reran that home movie in his mind: the three of them taking turns perforating the tenderest parts of a chicken with an unloaded hypodermic—his own unsteady hand wielding the syringe at a place where Sylvie's tears had moistened the plucked fowl. A grim beginning—and yet, the onset of J-P's diabetes marked the end of Sylvie's own mysterious series of illnesses; the witches' Sabbath they had spent puncturing an obscene bird was the last time Paul had seen her cry.

Sylvie appeared in the doorway (exactly as in Paul's movie,

behind J-P's back)—but dry-eyed now, composed, wearing an apron, her sweater sleeves pushed to the elbow. Paul remained perched on the toilet seat during the intimate ritual between mother and son. With the precision of a surgeon Sylvie first bathed her hands in alcohol then removed the glass syringe from the jar of ether with a pair of tweezers, careful not to touch the piston. She washed the syringe in alcohol and shook it dry (Paul had smashed one, trying that), then attached a fresh needle from the sterile pack; she rubbed the top of the insulin container with cotton dipped in alcohol, plunged the needle into the rubberoid opening and tilted the container toward the light. She drew out more than the prescribed units of insulin, tapped the syringe to eliminate an air bubble, then carefully pushed the plunger back to the mark. J-P was already holding his pajama sleeve as high as it would go, fearless (he was a veteran of a thousand injections), staring dreamily into the rainbow of his color chart.

As Sylvie pinched up the tiny mound of flesh between two fingers, Paul looked away. He stared out the window to the garden and thought about the childish argument J-P's diabetes had brought on:

"It's hereditary, the doctor said."

Like colic, thought Paul. "Well, there's never been a diabetic in my family."

"How do you know?"

"There's just never been."

"It has to be on your side. We have records of family three generations back, and never never has there been diabetes."

"But I just told you. There's no diabetes in my family either."

"You don't even know your family. And your mother believes in Christian Science—she would have denied she had it."

"Well, she didn't. She would have died if she had it."

"*Tu es bête.*"

"No sillier than you. The whole thing is silly. Why do you want to blame me for J-P's diabetes, like a strain of syphilis or something I passed on to him."

"I'm not blaming you. I just said diabetes is hereditary and nobody on my side has ever been diabetic."

"And I said there's never been diabetes in my family."

"*Tu es vraiment bête.*"

One of those pointless disputes that started from nothing, went nowhere, and before it fizzled out left both of them bitter, nourishing their newest grudge.

Paul kept his eyes averted and stared even deeper into the shadows of the garden as if to remove himself from this vaguely sexual ceremony between mother and son.

Perhaps the ether fumes had affected his brain: he saw (or thought he saw) an indistinct figure moving through the dried stalks of last summer's tomato vines. He had never seen the ghostly little girl anywhere but in Roquebrune— why had the apparition followed him here? He wanted to ask Sylvie to look, to confirm the phantom child outside, but he knew he could not share the vision with her. Christine, surreal as she was, belonged to him alone—in the way Jean-Paul had become, for now, his mother's son.

No, the shadowy figure was too tall for a child. And bent with age. He realized, just as the old crone moved out of sight, that it was Madame Roustan, en route to her rabbits via the *droit de passage.*

He returned to the bathroom ritual just as Sylvie withdrew

the needle, in time to see a tiny droplet of blood. Sylvie quickly rubbed the upper arm with cotton, as if erasing the experience from J-P's mind (but it was Paul whose legs went watery—J-P had long accepted the needle punctures as routine), and she was already discarding the used needle, rinsing the syringe under cold water: Sylvie had become a careful and efficient nurse as a natural extension of the mother's role. Paul, the father, remained baffled and afraid.

Despite a persistent optimism, Paul's fears were his undoing: dreams turned to nightmare, anxieties to disaster—only his daylight visions sustained him. A diabetic might go blind. Unattended diabetes could lead to coma, paralysis, brain damage, death. He brooded on these horrors each time the routine of injection came around. (Sylvie knew what must be done about the disability and did it.) To Paul's fear of heights, his dread of drowning, claustrophobia, paranoia, vertigo, he could add the fear of the sight of his own son's blood.

Seven

Her hair was still bound in the tight croissant, but she had taken her apron off and carried a drink in her hand. Sylvie never drank, but she drank now: a yellow liqueur, gentiane, made from mountain flowers—hardly a bracer, perhaps a token accompaniment to Paul's cognac.

"How's he doing in school?"

"He has good notes. Grades, I mean." She placed her drink on the coffee table, sat on the low sofa and lifted her arms to the back of her head in a way that stirred Paul's blood. She took a hairpin—just one—out of the croissant.

"He ask much about me?"

Paul had put on a spool of tape that spun out the soothing convolutions of "The Musical Offering." No matter what turn the conversation took, their words would have to compete with the art and sanity of Johann Sebastian Bach.

"Sometimes. I tell him you are working."

"What does he say to that?"

"It's the truth."

"Yes, but what does he think? About us."

"I don't know what he thinks. And I do not intend to discuss our—situation—with a seven-year old." She set to work bending the hairpin into a hook for a fragile red Christmas tree globe.

"Of course."

The drink had warmed him nicely, then neatly hollowed him out: a voluptuous warmth, a free-floating spin—he would have to watch his words, careful not to let the cognac speak for him. He did not want to become bullheaded or too blunt. He was capable of that, with a drink that went down too well. Or easing into his lighthearted offhand manner that he knew set Sylvie's teeth on edge.

After a moment in which Sylvie seemed to be going through an index file, she said: "His bed-wetting is worse."

"Of course." The diabetes only partly explained bed-wetting at seven. "He needs his father."

"He wet the bed when you were here."

"But you say it's worse now."

"It's the same, then. I mean, he still wets the bed."

"I see." He made a gesture with his glass, a careful gesture.

There was just enough light to keep the best shadows intact. The drink and the music and the wood fire set the mood. He put a twisted olive log into the blazing bed of pine cones and split oak, a log almost too beautiful to burn. The olive (he had told J-P at bedtime) was Athena's gift to mankind, and in Christian times the olive branch became a symbol of peace. Paul's mind was stuffed with a cluttered inventory of such oddments, and he fed this mostly useless information to his son, who would in turn (when least expected) recite the encyclopedic bits and pieces word for word, translated into French.

Sylvie dangled the Christmas tree ornament from its hook, to see if it would hold. Paul poured. The brandy bottle was shaped like a bowling pin, rich brown, sealed with brittle wax and a tricolor ribbon across the cork, twenty-five years old—just the kind of expensive gift Duff would give, the perfect drink on just so awkward an occasion.

Paul warmed the snifter in his hands, swirled it gently to stir up the fumes. The smell of brandy and woodsmoke were so agreeable he considered stubbing out his cigarette (Sylvie would be pleased: she had read the U.S. Surgeon General's Report and given up smoking; she claimed the smell of nicotine got into the draperies, even into her hair), but he went on smoking. They had begun the ritual tango around the several banal issues between them; for this he needed a drink in one hand, a cigarette in the other.

Sylvie got up and went to the tree to fasten the globe to a bare branch. Paul watched her carefully, as if expecting the delicate ornament to shatter and signal the end to a temporary truce. J-P's bedtime kiss still lingered in the corner of his mouth and Paul wanted the comforting silence to continue, share a portion of peace with his wife, offer her "The Musical Offering." But when she turned to him she was in tears.

Damn. This was her way to cry: from inside, without a

sound. It was worse than words. He was exasperated by these mysterious tears and she seemed to despise her own tearful outbursts as much as he did. Still, it had been so long since she wept—perhaps tears were a first step to something. He sat for a moment, helpless with no way to get to the heart of a tristesse not even she could define.

He came away from his cognac to be with her, still holding the cigarette, careful of the ash. He put an arm around her: "What is it?"

"It's all wrong, so much. I can't stand it. Even being touched."

"By me?" He released her, dismayed. "Is that it?"

"Things change, but you don't."

"What?"

"Change."

"What should I change?"

"Adjust, I mean."

"To what?"

"To things. To me."

True, she was changed. She had grown, if not beyond him, in some oblique direction of her own.

"I do adjust. Don't I?"

"No."

"Well, what? Tell me."

"You're not sensitive. To what happens. You're so—" she sought the word in English "—so complacent."

"I worry about things, too—if that's what you mean."

"But you don't do anything about it."

"About what?"

"The way things change."

"What's changed?"

"I am."

"True."

"But you're not. You're so complacent. Time passes and you just sit there."

He was standing. He started to put his arm around her, then remembered and brought it down.

"True, I'm out of touch sometimes. I'm wrong about things. A lot of things."

She turned away. A plea of *nolo contendere* was not allowed.

"O.K. In what way am I supposed to change?"

This brought on more tears.

"I *am* sensitive, even when I don't seem to be. I feel things, I hurt. I feel when you're hurt."

He could not cope with silent tears so he decided to risk putting his arm around her after all.

This was his own bed, their bed, the garden window open and a slice of moon across the sheet. Sylvie's hair was down out of the twist of croissant at last, her tears had dried. He touched her with those first tentative caresses as familiar as the bed itself. He grew quickly hard, pinched between his leg and hers.

"I don't have on—the thing."

"Oh?"

"I didn't put it in."

"You want to put it in?"

"I'd better."

She was right, of course. He remembered the bad time after the time they decided not to bother. The pain of waiting was a pleasure too. She went to the bathroom and he was alone for a moment. He softened and thought, what if? —but she was back in an instant, slightly chilled from the passage through the unheated hall. He warmed her and was aroused again. She responded slowly, in her fashion—somewhat distant, vaguely distracted, but acquiescent. His passion carried him beyond concern for her somewhat formal acceptance of his entry: when he thrust himself into the soft moist heart between her thighs she stiffened. He felt welcome only in the way of a paying guest. Still, she worked at it. She moved with him athletically enough, but he had lost her early. He altered the rhythm of his thrusts, but she was no longer there. Her flesh so enticed him he stayed with it, though he was, he knew, alone inside her, caressing himself.

"Go ahead," she said, "if you're ready." She, obviously, was not.

"Let's—"

"No. Go ahead."

He went ahead. The release, since it was solitary, was a guilty half pleasure—but a release all the same. For a moment with that sweet emptying spasm he was free. *La petite morte*, the French called it. The little death, before the big one.

Eight

She lay with her back to him (after the comic episode of his sneeze and popping out of her like a cork) but close enough that he could curl jack-knifed against her, his knees in the back hollow of hers. He placed his hand against her stomach and felt the chilled flesh from the cold-water douche (cold water to kill off the little *grimpeurs*, the climbers that struggled upstream like salmon headed for the tranquil mating pool, like Paul swimming against the cataract to make it with his wife); he moved his hand to her breast and felt the comforting heartbeat inside. If only he could sleep to her heartbeat, as he had done so many thousands of nights before. Her heartbeat was steady, her breathing regular; she slept—he was the insomniac now.

He badly wanted a cigarette but dared not move, afraid to undo the interlocking puzzle of their two bodies touching. He lay on the wet spot from their lovemaking, his hip in the puddle of sperm, and he eased his free hand under her pillow searching for the worn towel she kept there to wipe up the sticky aftermath; his hand touched only the brittle plastic of an emergency flashlight, in case the electricity failed. It occurred to him the wet spill touched his scar, the place where she had plunged a pair of scissors, and he tried to make something significant of this—the spilling of blood and sperm—but gave up on it. He slid one numb foot from under hers and felt the needles. A cigarette, a drink—he thought of the expensive cognac Duff had given him (typically, three days before Amazing Growth collapsed). Should he try for another brandy, and risk waking her? No. Poor timing, poor politics.

There was a time when he could have projected himself into her dreams as easily as into her body, but not now. Were her nightmares so different from his own? Once he had had access to her dread as well as her delight, but no longer. And even then there had been enough mystery to her to keep him forever enchanted. But too much mystery now. Those things she would not talk about—then and now—were the serious hurts that would not heal. When she stabbed him with those scissors she had injured herself far deeper than his negligible wound. Paul had kept the bandaged place hidden from her and never referred to the incident, but Sylvie staggered through a week of anguish and brooding guilt until at last she asked to be taken to a hospital.

Before their marriage she had questioned him closely

about his health, a curious interrogation. Paul believed the marriage vows adequately covered the prospect of sickness and health, and "till death do us part" was sufficient unto the day.

"I do not intend to marry a man who needs a nurse."

"Never fear. I'm in top shape."

"What does 'top shape' mean?"

"Means 'in the pink,' means I'm healthy as a horse."

After she filed away the new idioms she asked him: "Do you ever get depressed?"

"Sure. Doesn't everybody?"

She did not mean depressed, she meant *depressed*.

"Maybe not that bad."

It was time to confess those hidden flaws, and she was leading up to a weakness of her own. In all fairness (not *all* fairness, Paul reflected, but fair enough) she admitted to a serious depressive episode in her adolescence. She then waited for Paul to outline his own shady medical history, but all he could come up with was a close brush with appendicitis and a crushing, transient, teenage despair over being too light for the football team.

That was not what Sylvie meant. She had undergone psychoanalysis, briefly, and wanted Paul to know. Paul knew at least fifteen people who had been—or still were—in analysis. It was, he assured her, the twentieth-century thing to do.

"My psychoanalyst was a woman doctor who looked very much like my mother—which didn't help."

How could it? thought Paul, since Sylvie's mother looked like a predatory fish.

To please Dr. Leiden—who was from a German-speaking canton—Sylvie free-associated in German, a language she spoke fluently but loathed, and was too shy to switch to French—"so the sessions came to nothing, and I quit."

What she did not tell Paul until long after their marriage was that soon after the failed analysis she drifted into a crippling melancholia and spent the summer of her seventeenth year at a sanitarium in Berne.

Paul saw no other way but to ask Duff for a leave of absence.

"What the hell's up?"

"It's Sylvie, she's not well."

Duff probed until he got the story out of Paul, then recommended a top man in Nice.

"No use going to a hack when it's a question of the mind."

Dr. Malsain's office was over the Florentine arcades around the Place Massena: three rooms of Louis XV furniture and IBM gadgetry, with a view of the Galeries Lafayette. An electroencephalograph took up most of one wall in the largest room, and there was a small, intimate salon equipped with an adjustable chair—like a dentist's chair with straps, or something useful at Sing Sing—for out-patient shock treatment. As soon as Paul passed through the pretentious *mise en scène* to a receptionist wearing platform shoes and pearls, he suspected this was just another Riviera con. By the time he had disengaged himself from the doctor's swift shifty handshake he was fighting against the impulse to call the whole thing off. But Sylvie was impressed (or needed to be impressed), and Paul succumbed to Sylvie's need.

Paul's only experience with doctors was the hernia checkup and V.D. lectures during Basic Training in the Army. He nourished an innate skepticism of the medical profession inherited from his parents: his father had been a tough-minded disbeliever in governments and God, who pulled his own teeth with a pair of pliers to avoid the fuss and expense of dentistry (and died of electrocution repairing a short-circuit in a rainstorm). His mother was a Christian Scientist.

Sylvie came out of another tradition, and she maintained an almost religious belief in the omniscience of doctors. She was subdued in their presence, and her natural independence of spirit disappeared. In Paul's opinion Europeans were conditioned to regard the medical profession as a distinguished order of hard-working saints, and European doctors encouraged this reverence until they began to believe in the myth themselves.

Doctor Malsain saw the two of them together, then Sylvie alone, then Paul alone. Paul was unhappy with the man's pink, twitching rabbit face.

"Your wife," piped the doctor in his flutey French, "is suffering from severe depression."

Paul had trained himself, in France, to be patient with this kind of runaround. He gave no sign. The doctor was possibly aware he was in the presence of a nonbeliever, and grew distracted in the silence that followed: he pressed his fingertip obsessively to the point of a ballpoint pen. Paul wanted to tell him he was getting ink on his fingers. *What is this man's problem?*

"The result, in my opinion, of a postpartum psychosis."

Which sounded legitimate enough, maybe even correct— whatever it meant. After a few fussy mannerisms terminating in a throat caress that left an ink stain on his Adam's apple, the doctor recommended a *cure de sommeil*. Somehow the term *cure de sommeil* sounded therapeutic, even life-saving, to Paul's untrained ear. And Sylvie was delighted to hear of a treatment that promised an unlimited stretch of blessed sleep. Doctor Malsain was on the staff of a private clinic in the suburbs of Nice, and later when Paul told Duff that Sylvie was a patient at St. François, Duff said, "Fantastic. Brigitte Bardot took a rest cure there."

Madame Chaix came down from Geneva to take the household in hand but immediately broke the wrist of that hand trying to change a lightbulb from a shaky upturned wastebasket. She settled down to a month's knitting with a cast on one arm. Fortunately the baby had made the switch from breast to bottle with no trauma and was beginning to sleep a normal night through. Madame Chaix had confiscated Paul's favoriate armchair and sat there most of the day producing booties and miniature sweaters for J-P while Paul handled her requests for coffee and apéritifs. She was obliged to hold one rapierlike needle rigidly upright in the broken hand and knit around it, as if fencing. She threw out an occasional inquiry, but she had grown deaf in one ear and Paul could never remember which one it was.

"*Tu crois que le bébé a faim?*"

"I just fed him," replied Paul.

"*Pardon?*"

"I just fed him."

"*Je n'entends pas.*"

"I just fed him."

"*Ah, bon.*"

Paul and his mother-in-law took alternating trips to St. François: when it was Paul's turn, Madame Chaix stayed with the baby. However, visiting hours with Sylvie meant little more than an evening's bedside watch. He brushed a fly from her sleeping face, studied the finger swollen around the wedding band, watched the narcotic fluid drip relentlessly like a Chinese water torture through a plastic tube, then into a vein by way of a needle clipped to Sylvie's bruised forearm. A nurse informed Paul the patient was awake part of the day for hospital routine: the bidet, a trip to the WC, an occasional tray—otherwise she was nourished and sustained by the liquids suspended at her bedside, flowing into her through tubes. There were dark hollows under her closed eyes, a rash across her forehead. By the fourth visit Paul noticed she twitched in her sleep. Another time she groaned aloud.

Whenever Paul tried to contact Dr. Malsain at the hospital, the word was inevitably, "*Le docteur est parti*," he had just left. When Paul telephoned his office in Nice the receptionist answered and said the doctor was at lunch or in conference, or he got a recorded reply—in English and French—with the request that he leave his number, which would be recorded and the doctor would call him back. It was as if the doctor had disappeared inside his elaborate office machinery, and Paul was ready to take a taxi to Place Massena and storm into the office when he did, finally, reach the doctor by telephone, to learn: "*Tout va bien, tout va bien.*" All's well hell, thought Paul. Should he rip the tube from its rack, pull the bloody needle from her arm, bring her back among the living? But Paul was alone in his panic. The nurses chirped birdlike assurances and the head nurse hinted that Brigitte Bardot had undergone the same treatment. Madame Chaix had miraculously run into Dr. Malsain at St. François (twice), had great confidence in him (was charmed, in fact) and carried home the doctor's catchword: "*Tout va bien.*"

In the beginning of Sylvie's hospitalization Paul built up a romantic fable around the *cure de sommeil* as a modern replay of *Sleeping Beauty*. In three weeks, when Malsain's spell had run its course, Paul would be the prince who awakened *la belle au bois dormant* from the long sleep. It was not to be. Madame Chaix was at the hospital when the cure came to an end; she was at Sylvie's bedside when the tubes and drugs were wheeled away: she called Paul to tell him all was well, and he could come pick them up in a taxi anytime.

Paul arrived to find his princess waiting, propped up by a nurse and his mother-in-law. Her streetclothes hung awkwardly on the diminished frame; her face was haggard, almost unfamiliar (she seemed to have aged, and Paul saw her mother in her changed face). Her eyes did not focus—when she moved to kiss him she missed and kissed his ear.

For weeks following the cure Sylvie could not rouse herself; she remained drugged still, without appetite or interest, drifting from room to room trying to remember what she meant to do or to find a reason to do something. The long siege of sleep had turned his wife into a shadow, increased her despair, brought her anguish to a higher pitch. Dr. Malsain informed him by phone (his appointments calendar was filled) that one could expect a certain "reaction" these first days. Was Madame taking her Elavil as prescribed?

They gave up on the evasive Malsain and switched to a neurologist in Cannes who had long, flowing gray hair, wore lemon-colored slacks and drove a Maserati. Dr. Gaillard tried Sylvie on Valium for ten days, changed the Elavil to Equanil and added Seconal to help her sleep ("Sleep," Paul insisted, "is no longer the problem.") They dropped Gaillard and turned to Dr. Hoquet, who favored Anafranil and Tofranil, Seresta and Temesta. (Paul had learned that no French doctor gave fewer than four drugs per prescription.) Dr. Prochêne was next, a follower of Coué, who proposed a series of thirty-six hypnotic sessions; then they went to Dr. Pauvret, a resentful Algerian *pied-noir* who talked politics for half an hour and charged five hundred francs for the initial interview, which was their last.

The only doctor Paul liked and trusted in the whole colorful series was Dr. Blancheneige, an elderly, fatherly, old-fashioned M.D. His slow-motion approach was a relief (he reminded Paul of Lionel Barrymore as Dr. Kildare), but he was forgetful—he could seldom remember Sylvie's name, and was never sure what he was treating her for. Sylvie was with him only six weeks before his retirement when Blancheneige, Jr., a shock-treatment adept, came down from Montpellier to take over the practice.

Eventually Sylvie got in touch with the long-forgotten Dr. Grandjacquot in St. Raphael, whose practice had languished during his illness (or floated away on new tides of popularity to other shores) and who treated *"le corps entier."* He recorded Sylvie's medical history on tape and prescribed a rainbow of homeopathic pills the size of birdseed that had to be taken at precise intervals: pink on the hour, white on the half-hour, blue on the quarter-hour—which meant Sylvie was forever glancing at her watch; she kept an egg timer ticking in her purse if she had to leave the apartment.

What were the pills *for?* Paul wanted to ask, but to question their value brought on a nervous crisis bordering on hysteria. She was often in tears. The relentless schedule of multicolored pills created a new anguish, fresh anxieties, Paul was helpless to assuage.

"I can't remember if I took my pills at ten-fifteen."

"It won't matter, for once."

"It *does* matter. It has to be *right.*"

"Then take some extra blues in fifteen minutes."

"That's worse. I can't do that. It has to be *right.*"

She wept against his shirtfront and was vaguely comforted. He was her sanctuary when frustration became too keen to bear, her dependable last resort.

Meanwhile she would take advice from anyone but him. She recited her symptoms and discussed her treatment with the mailman, taxi drivers, cashiers and the concierge. She worried about the ozone and hormones and minimum daily requirements of protein and vitamin B. She had got hold of Adelle Davis in English and Gaylord Hauser in French and began serving wheat germ, blackstrap molasses and *riz complet*. At lunch they sprinkled yeast on their soup and ate *crudités*: cold beets, carrot sticks, cold potatoes sliced thin with radishes and onions in olive oil. They gave up pork after a trichinosis scare at the Paris *abattoirs* and abandoned veal when Sylvie learned that calves were injected with chemicals to fatten them artificially. She made cutlets from crushed nuts and paté from soya and chopped mushrooms. Apples had to be scrubbed with soap and water because they might have come from trees sprayed with poison; watercress was to be avoided since streams had become polluted with urine from infected sheep.

Sylvie scrutinizing a tomato held up to the light reminded Paul of Lady Macbeth.

She was prey to every passing infection: a series of colds, earache, laryngitis and at least one devastating grippe every winter. A street sweeper told her about the effectiveness of raw onion against respiratory ailments, and a hairdresser explained the benefits of sea water inhaled through one nostril and expelled through the other. Sylvie bought cartons of sea water in glass containers, those infernal French ampoules that had to be sawed open with miniature hacksaws without spilling the liquid or swallowing splinters of glass. It was called Plasma de Quinton. "Are you sure," Paul asked, "it isn't just tap water and salt?" She was not amused. (She was never amused any more.) Nothing Paul could dream up would distract her from *le corps entier*. When he suggested a restaurant meal for a change, she was certain to refuse, fearful of food that came from any kitchen but her own. She was restless at movies, or tearful—often they had to leave before the film was over. Once, to relieve a hectic day of disaster (J-P was teething, the toilet failed to flush), Paul opened a bottle of Moet & Chandon—but Sylvie put her champagne glass to one side and managed to sour Paul's wine by reciting statistics on liver damage.

They made love, despite all—and Sylvie was an ardent partner in bed. Their lovemaking was frequent, as if to make up for everything else; her response could be passionate: frantic sometimes, almost desperate. Paul had come to believe in this one large hopeful outlet, until Sylvie once blandly confessed she had read "in Simone de Beauvoir or someplace" that sex was the ideal way for a woman to maintain perfect hormone balance.

Doctors treating his wife were rivals from whom he could not win her. Their prescriptions were billets-doux, and the casual request "*Revenez en dix jours*" was a love tryst in medical code. Could you sue, in France, for alienation of affection? The affairs never lasted long enough for Paul to be jealous of any single doctor (Sylvie dropped the relationship too quickly for that)—it was the entire French medical establishment that was suspect. Malsain, her original seducer, was the first to set spinning a prayer wheel of uppers and downers, sedatives and antidepressants, to introduce her to the half-world of dependency and hypochondria—aided and abetted by each succeeding doctor who wooed her and held her, for a time, in an embrace that explored her flesh for infirmity and tranquilized her to his will; even Gaylord Hauser (a Hollywood Don Juan operating overseas) had broken into his home via bottles of yeast pills and packages of wheat germ embossed with his insidious name and trademark; or that anonymous herbalist in Arles who sent her essence of lavender to gargle and hooked her on *l'argile qui guerit,* the clay that heals, powdered clay to be cooked into mud and applied anywhere, a healing kiss against any pain (or swallowed, like a love potion); even the butcher across the street, in all innocence, talking Sylvie into compresses of boiled cabbage leaves applied to her breasts to keep a chest cold from becoming pneumonia.

Invariably she came back to Paul after each brief flirtation —he was the healer she needed most whenever the newest fad failed. Then came an end to it all: J-P had diabetes. Sylvie's symptoms cleared up overnight—her physical disabilities were healed, her depression disappeared and the only tears she shed were for her son.

Paul could not sleep, partly because her accusation—vague as it was—was probably true. She had changed. He had not been sensitive to the change in her, and now it might be too late. He was the same daydreaming American she had known all along—his French had gotten no better, his outlook no worse, *Made in U.S.A.* written across his face—but Sylvie had overcome a crippling handicap and become new. (He thought how often he would find a withered slice of onion she had pressed to her ear, in bed next day, and two hot-water bottles grown cold, and he recalled the mail-order Damart nightgown she wore then, to keep warm, unpleasant synthetic material that gave off sparks when they made love.) How lustily she slept. She could plunge into the heart of sleep without him, their roles reversed. She had left him behind at some milestone far back, and he was the troubled, uncertain, searching, unfortunate now.

Paul was beginning to believe Sylvie knew what she wanted, and what she wanted had nothing to do with him.

Coréine, Codeine, Catalgine, Algésal. Ticking off the inventory of those troubled years kept him awake far into the night. Flubilar, Lysivit, Transfusine. He considered the remaining traces of Sylvie's former illnesses—the bottles, thermometers, compresses, pills, suppositories, inhalers, salves, capsules and powdered clay that still overflowed the medicine cabinet or were stored in roped cartons in the *cave* (for Sylvie never threw anything away, and Paul had total recall for such trivia)—counting the pharmaceuticals like sheep: Demerol, Dimagin, Bactrim, Intetrix, Sympathyl, Sulfarlem, Primpéarn, Phisohex, Gastroléna, Vogalène, Leucodine, Sedibaine, Anti-, Exo-, Meto-, min, man, med, me.

Nine

The uneasy question lingered just beyond the comfort threshold. *Where am I?* He touched himself, his sex, then the soft warm hollow where she had been—alarm, confusion —*where is she?* Another solitary morning and no wife.

As he dressed he caught sight of Sylvie on the terrace under a chill beginning sun: she was doing her Yoga, the *salut au soleil*, wrapped in a blanket. Paul put a cigarette between his lips and searched for matches. The drawer to her night table was partly open; he was certain there were no matches there, but he looked into the drawer anyway. (He hated this trait in himself but invariably gave in to it.) There was a letter from his mother-in-law he did not bother to read —her cramped handwriting and abbreviated French took forever to decipher—but he did glance through two items Sylvie had clipped from *Express*: one, an article about an artificial pancreas for diabetics; the other (he winced) explaining the new divorce laws in France. He folded the clippings away with hands turned suddenly cold. There was a can of vaginal spray, a nail file and a flower of crushed Kleenex —but no matches. He did come across a folded photostat of his last will and testament, signed at the consulate in Nice, and seeing it gave him the same spooked feeling he had when he signed it.

He found matches in the living room and considered playing the Bach tape again but thought the sound of music might disturb Sylvie's exercise in contemplation. (Since she was not searching for salvation from the East, her transfer from Medicine to Yoga passed with no noticeable trauma. Sylvie's Swiss Protestant background kept her from expecting *karma:* the practice of Yoga, according to her testimony, was nothing more than a disciplined way to concentrate, keep fit and fight the ravages of time.)

J-P, still wearing his urine-stained pajamas, gave Paul a kiss *bon jour* in the bathroom. This might have been any one of a thousand mornings in their family cycle: Paul shaving (but with Sylvie's underarm razor, with a blade he had sharpened inside a water tumbler) and J-P under the shower washing the night's bed-wetting away. All was as it should be—or appeared so—but on J-P's face was the troubled wondering at the new order of things; his expression seemed to ask: Is Papa really home to stay? Papa, shaving around his cigarette, wondered too.

In the kitchen a saucepan of insulin needles boiled on the electric burner, the polished floor tiles gleamed up at him like a *Plaisir de la Maison* ad—he would have to watch his cigarette ash. He searched for coffee, but found none; he even checked in his old Peugeot coffee grinder for perhaps a little coffee residue he could boil up, but no trace remained. Sylvie no longer drank coffee: she made tea from mint, thyme or eucalyptus leaves. He settled for orange juice, and for one reckless moment was tempted to spike his juice from the vodka bottle he had seen last night in the liquor cabinet, but resisted, and drank the juice down straight.

From the kitchen window he could see Sylvie standing on her head. (Her Armenian guru had convinced her the pose was ideal for sluggish circulation.) Sylvie's brief romance with Zen Buddhism had come to nothing: she found the wizened Zen master in Antibes a senile bore, with his vicious bamboo rod and those silly Zen riddles called *koan*. She left after two sessions and joined a Yoga class in Grasse, taught by an Armenian adept who seemed to be just one lesson ahead of his students. In contrast to her doctor phase, here Sylvie was in control—she pointed out inconsistencies in technique and corrected her Yoga teacher's French. Paul took a sly delight in her conversion; besides, how could he be jealous of Buddha? The terrace was in full sun now, and Sylvie used the blanket as a headrest. What lovely legs, thought Paul.

He set out three sea-green ceramic cups and saucers (listed, he recalled, on Sylvie's *séparation de biens*), and sliced open a Tunisian grapefruit—half each for Sylvie and J-P (one aesthetic pleasure of breakfast abroad, the citrus was stenciled with a brand name in Arabic, instead of SUNKIST).

"Bonjour."

"Hi."

"The sun is shining," announced Sylvie.

Paul pondered several responses to this but could come up with nothing better than "It certainly is."

Sylvie took the needles from the saucepan and put three eggs in the boiling water. Three eggs, for the three of them. Paul contemplated the number 3 while she weighed J-P's bread on a postal scale: twenty grams. When J-P came in they sat down to breakfast together, a family of three.

Paul's senses (his appetite, particularly) were heightened

by the significance of the scene: their first morning together in months. What bread ever tasted fresher?—a new-baked *bâtard* delivered by the baker only ten minutes ago. (It was still too hot to slice, so they each in turn tore a piece from the loaf.) The eggs were from Madame Roustan's chickens next door. And Sylvie had taken the exquisite trouble to carve the servings of butter into pale yellow rosettes. Even the thyme tea (an insipid infusion at best) tasted right, seemed fitting—the thyme, after all, was from the rim of woods behind the house. The Phantom Inspector awarded his own home three stars.

Sylvie was going through the mail.

"Sécurité Sociale has gone up."

"The cost?"—Paul was trying to sound practical—"or the benefits?"

"The cost." She passed an envelope across the table to him: *Union de Recouvrement des Cotisations de Sécurité Sociale et d'Allocations Familiales.*

Paul studied the figures with all the concentration he could muster. The document was as mysterious as the Code Civil he had sworn to at their wedding. Now what? It was a bill—for how much, he did not know—but he knew she knew he could not pay it.

"Yes," he said, and handed it back to her.

"I do not see how people can live."

Paul found it impossible to reply to this and was happy when J-P held up one finger, a way of asking to speak—as he would have done at school—and of not interrupting adults. They both turned to him.

"If the gravity holds people on *la terre* what holds on the gravity?"

"Gravity," said Sylvie, "is a force, like electricity."

"Yes," said Paul, somehow relieved.

Then J-P counted aloud the days until Christmas vacation, chattered about the *pétanque* tournament scheduled for recess, asked if Athena who gave the olive branch was a man or a woman god.

"Can Papa take me to school?" he asked his mother.

"We will both take you to school," said Sylvie, and she handed the car keys to Paul.

She even sat in the front with him as he drove. This was an unbroken chain of good fortune; Paul feared to examine the portents too closely. The trouble with being the Phantom Inspector was a professional habit of summing up trivia: looking for minuscule stains on restaurant napkins, analyzing the contents of the soup. Let it be, he warned himself—stop keeping score.

As the Opel surged up the Chemin du Paradis Paul thought about the word *paradis:* paradise, pronounced parody.

"If the gravity should go off as does electricity during a strike would we all turn into astronauts?"

"It won't go off," Paul assured him.

Gravity. That was the answer to Sylvie's question about how people manage to live: they hang on. Gravity was not subject to storm or a strike by Eléctricité de France. It was a natural force, like love.

J-P wore the official institutional blue smock and carried a set of *boules* in a leather strap. He kissed his father through the car window and went off to the schoolyard hive, bare knees pumping, plastic schoolbag bouncing from his shoulders. As soon as he approached his schoolmates he went immediately into *Midi* French—Paul delighted in the comic intonation of his son's southern speech. J-P could move in and out of accents as easily as changing hats. Yes, the boy was French, and thus more Sylvie than himself—but he had willingly given up that share in J-P's character so that his son could have this pastel-tinted childhood in place of Paul's own grade-school souvenir in gray. At this safe distance Paul need not resurrect that winter-dreary public school in Cincinnati—it was enough to recall the smell and the cold and the lack of color.

The school in Ys was part of the village *mairie*, the town hall—a single classroom on one side of the mayor's office, the PTT (post office, telephone and telegraph) on the other. The plane trees around the schoolyard were trimmed for winter; next spring the bare knobby branches would sprout again (a miracle, from the look of them now), and a canopy of delicate new green would shade the playground from the fierce southern sun.

Clusters of birds were attracted by the shrill cries of the children and shrieked a cacophony from the amputated trees; pigeons strutted along the PTT roof tiles and roosted in the ancient clockface over the *mairie*, while the schoolmaster's tiger cat sat in a windowsill surveying the flutter with an eager but cynical French eye.

Surveying the scene, too, were the ancients of the village in wrinkled blue denim seated at the base of the war monument across the *place*, above their heads the brass scroll inscribed with the names of the sons of the commune who had given their lives on the field of honor. The old men were guardians of the word and the myth. They had been there when Paul and Sylvie and J-P first came to Ys, watching the newcomers fit themselves into the life of the village. As fixed in time as the clockface over the *mairie* (the clock had no hands, the chimes never chimed, the pigeons roosted there in peace), the old men were perpetual witnesses to anything that happened or would ever happen here. We belong here now, Paul wanted to shout to them—but they, like the cat, were content to wait and watch.

Sylvie had said something twice and was staring at Paul as if he were deaf.

"Sorry," said Paul, "the birds make such a racket."

"I asked you to go into the mairie with me, for your signature."

His stomach turned cold: "Sign what?"

"I thought I told you. To take Jean-Paul to Switzerland for Christmas."

"You never said anything about Switzerland."

"I thought I told you last night. His grandmother offers him a ski holiday. For Christmas."

"Your mother?" Paul regretted the sound of his own voice.

"He would benefit from a holiday, the doctor said. The mountain air is good for him. And you know how he loves to ski."

"For Christmas? What about me?"

"I never keep you from him. Did I ever keep you from him?"

"You are now."

"For a ski holiday, that the doctor recommends. And his grandmother offers." Sylvie's face began to harden, her voice to rise: "Anyway, he wants to go. And I want him to go."

"Good," said Paul, with nothing good in the sound of it, "It's settled then."

"You have to sign the permission papers," said Sylvie quickly. She looked away.

"What's that?"

"Children can't cross the border of France without the signed permission of the father."

"But you're going with him."

"Yes, but you have to sign."

"I see." She could do this. (His mouth fell open, and he clamped it shut.) She could telephone him, woo him, sleep with him and boil his breakfast egg—then do this. For a signature, all along. The windshield blurred red at the edges; the trees, the *mairie*, the schoolchildren turned watery.

He could not look at her, and there was nothing to say unless he cursed. He played with his anger, toyed with his hurt without uttering a word of it. His face could tell her all she needed to know.

He understood scissors now, and as he drew himself inside the invisible cape of the Phantom Inspector and got out of the car he thought how he might have used a pair.

He left the car door hanging open like a broken wing and strode across the *place* past the eyes of the ancient witnesses of Ys. He was almost at the bus stop in front of the Toison d'Or before he realized there would be no bus till noon. He had no money for a cab, if there had been a cab—and the driver of a delivery truck with a tank of live trout was headed in the opposite direction.

A perverse fate had done him in again and turned another dilemma into farce. His keen piercing anger (like scissors) carried him for half the hike to Grasse, an hour's walk from Ys, but for the final minutes of it he heard only the *Midi* accent of his son, saw visions of his wife's exquisite legs.

Ten

Chère Papa:

Here it snows. I have practice my flute douce chaque matin after toothbrush. My ski is butter. I ski presque comme

Maman. Miniclub give chocolat for the best ski and Maman changes me shooing gomme (sans sucre) for chocolat.

Je t'embrasse, Jean-Paul

In matters of protocol Sylvie was scrupulously honest, compulsively fair. She had taken J-P to Switzerland after all (the card was from Leysin), but she had made him write Papa first thing. Had she bluffed her way across the border without a document signed by Paul—or had she pretended to be a widow?

Paul was having a cognac after breakfast, the earliest yet. On the strength of it he had decided to go to Leysin too, but he would need money, which meant confronting Grimwald with cognac on his breath. His employer could not abide sloppy personal lives. Is my personal life sloppy? Paul asked himself. "Yes," he replied aloud.

Paul had neglected to tell Grimwald he and Sylvie were living apart. Whenever Grimwald asked him, "What kind of car is that you drive?" and Paul told him an Opel Kadett, Grimwald would say, "It sounds like a lemon." Paul had also neglected to tell him that Sylvie had the car.

"What's the matter with it this time?"

Paul kept inventing repairs: "Transmission, I think," or, "I think it just needs a tune-up."

"There's no substitute for quality," Grimwald always said, and Paul was obliged to agree. Grimwald drove a chocolate-colored Mercedes-Benz.

With the help of a second cognac (a small one, just enough amber to wet the bottom of the glass) he typed the last two pages of next month's Phantom Inspector column. It was an uninspired report on glass blowing in Biot; Paul had already been paid for the piece, so the only incentive for finishing it was to have something in hand when he went to Grimwald for an advance.

Lacking wheels, the Phantom Inspector had to cover those tourist attractions within a smaller radius of Roquebrune. He grappled with the idiosyncracies of public transport: obsolete bus schedules, SNCF strikes, temperamental taxi drivers (if there were any). When pressed or somewhat desperate, he resorted to the Hertz car rental service in Monte Carlo; but Grimwald was inclined to examine expense-account vouchers in the light of his nostalgia for the day when you could get a two-star meal at a restaurant in Antibes for under nine francs. Thus Paul felt honor bound to return the vehicle to the Hertz garage before the Cinderella hour when another day's rate would automatically take effect.

He stuffed the manuscript into his plastic Monoprix briefcase trying to decide which way to travel: take the 9:15 autocar to Menton and change for the bus to Monte Carlo? Or walk down the endless steps of the Escalier Saft and hail the Monte Carlo bus on the Grande Corniche? The bus to Menton was roundabout but would conserve his strength for the conference with Grimwald. This meant traveling north-northeast to reach south-southwest; however, since his ultimate destination was Switzerland, a straight line was not the shortest distance between two points.

The offices of the *Guide* were on the seventeenth floor of the twenty-story Société des Investissements de Monaco building on Avenue J.F. Kennedy, and Grimwald's view was the very same spectacle Princess Grace enjoyed from the palace window: a ragged shoreline blighted with bulbous monster gas tanks, a railroad siding of idle, rusted freight cars, a stadium, a zoo and a brewery.

Paul looked out on this with the cold eye of the Phantom

Inspector while Miss Bishop (a British import) made tea on the top of her switchboard.

"He's on both phones, Paul," she said proudly (for it was seldom the two trunk lines were in use), "but I'll buzz you in the moment he finishes."

She passed him a cup of tea, and he swallowed the Life-Saver he had been sucking to cover the smell of cognac. Grimwald, now in his sixties, had never married. "I never married, myself," Grimwald always said, but if he had, Paul imagined he would have married somebody like Miss Bishop who would have made of their marriage an enterprise as carefully organized and coolly functional as the multigraph mailing system for *Grimwald's Guide* subscribers. Sweet, devoted, efficient Miss Bishop—somewhat past retirement age, she once told him: "I'm a workhorse, I'll die with my boots on." (She will, too, thought Paul, wearing her rainy-day boots. Miss Bishop carried a black umbrella, in Monte Carlo, to work—there it was, propped against a filing cabinet.)

She tucked her hair and ears into a dictation headset and took a last loving sip of tea. Her pert unwrinkled face was a bland mask of talcum powder, with a slash of orange lipstick to frame her large artificial teeth. What was her love life like? She kept her comfortable bosom securely encased in something with ribbing that showed through her dowdy blouses. And she kept her thin sparrow's legs quite tightly together, thank you. Paul assumed the extent of Miss Bishop's carnal pleasure in life had been inserting switchboard plugs into holes and pulling them out again with a sigh.

"You may go in now, Paul."

Paul went in. Whatever mood you carried into Grimwald's office inevitably blended into blue. The windows were tinted like the no-glare windshields in tour buses.

"Paul?" Grimwald's eyesight was not what it should be.

Paul tried to make his hand rigid enough to survive the old man's military handshake but was not quick enough this time and got his hand crushed again. "Sit you down, my boy."

He sat in the deceptive leather chair that deflated discouragingly under his weight. His knees rose almost to shoulder level, and he stared up at Grimwald between his legs.

Grimwald was a workhorse, too. (Hard work, he always said, never hurt anybody.) He worked in his shirt sleeves, but with his necktie pulled tight: he was slightly flushed, either because of the necktie or with the pleasure of having dealt with two simultaneous phone calls. He leaned forward, his hands clamped together like gears. What huge knuckles the man has, thought Paul. A big man with a sunburned bald spot and milk-blue eyes, he ran the *Guide* "with a sense of the past, a knowledge of the present and an instinct for the future." He modeled himself on Ruskin, Baedeker and Nostradamus.

There was a cup of cold tea on the desk, but no ashtray in sight. Paul badly needed a cigarette.

The direct approach was Grimwald's way, so as soon as the old man cleared a channel of communications across his desk (pushed galleys and correspondence to one side, tossed his scribbled legal pad on top of the stack, disengaged himself from the snap-coil wire of one of the telephones) Paul plunged in.

"I thought of going to Switzerland, and I need a small advance."

He watched the stone face for any sign but saw none.

"How small?"

For a moment it seemed Grimwald was on the way to a smile, but the illusion lasted only an instant, and the twitch

at the corner of his mouth could have been a wince. Paul
blundered on.

"I thought I might do a piece on skiing." Paul abhorred
skis, skiing and the ski set.

"We just published Roger's 'Go-Go Snow Places' in No-
vember."

"I was thinking of a different slant, a special. The package-
tour crowd. There's a Club des Voyageurs hotel in Leysin,
and I thought—"

"Paul, Paul." A bad sign, saying his name twice. "You
know me, Paul, I always shoot from the hip. I very much
doubt you have given this proposal sufficient thought to
justify an expensive venture outside your home territory."

To shoot from the hip then, Paul said, "Yes, well, the
idea—so far—is somewhat off the top of my head, I admit.
Frankly, I need to make the trip for other, ah, personal,
reasons. So to speak." Paul slumped, then rallied and tried
to rise out of the depths of the leather chair: "But as soon
as I get into the feeling of the place, see the scene first hand
—you know: interview the brass, talk to the guests, take a
test run on some of the slopes—"

Grimwald raised one hand like a traffic signal.

"Hold on, fella—let me say something, and I mean this
more in a fatherly way than your employer talking—but
your so-called personal reasons for making this trip interest
me more (that's not to say I'm trying to pry) than your
idea to do a feature piece on a ski resort."

Why did he always feel like a truant schoolboy in Grimwald's presence?

"I really wouldn't want to go into it. Into that aspect. It's
a family thing."

"Your wife is Swiss, isn't she?"

"Yes, she is."

He wanted Paul to know he could put two and two together.

"I never married, myself," said the old man, and he began to talk in that slow, painful methodical way of his. Paul pictured him wearing an eyeshade and suspenders—and if he wore suspenders he would be snapping them now, he thought. Grimwald was preparing to tell the story of his life. Paul had already heard it—from Duluth to Monaco, the hard way. His first job, apprentice to an undertaker, he earned fifteen dollars per week.

"You want to know where I slept nights?" Paul knew the whole depressing tale, but Grimwald did not wait for his reply. "I slept in a coffin. And frankly I never slept better in my life."

As he sank deeper into the chair, Paul sank inside. He was slipping down, down through the chair, the floor, sinking seventeen storys deep, all the way to ground-floor Société des Investissements de Monaco and out to sea.

"I've been down and out," Grimwald went on, "and I've been sitting on top of the world, and if there's one lesson I learned in this school of hard knocks and soft soap—and I offer it to you, Paul, for whatever it's worth—we don't always get what we bargained for in life, and what we bargained for is not always worth having."

Food for thought, but small nourishment to a man who needed three hundred dollars in a hurry.

Grimwald hooked his fingers together again on the desk top—not quite an attitude of prayer, more a hint of helplessness in the face of the facts of life—and this time when he flipped his thumbs up it meant thumbs down.

Miss Bishop had taken off her headset in such a rush a strand of gray hair was strung out over one ear. Her eyes were large and liquid in the stark white face—a tragic look, a seated Stabat Mater. She did—except for the earphones at her neck instead of a cameo—remind him of his mother.

"He left the intercom open, I couldn't help but hear."

Paul dismissed the breach of privacy with an offhand gesture—he might have done the same himself.

"He's not an ungenerous person, Paul, or spiteful. When you've been with him as long as I have, you'll know."

Paul did not intend to be with him for as long as she had. What he resented was not so much the droning platitudes as knowing *Grimwald's Guide* had to lose money to make money: it was only part of the old man's complicated inter-locking enterprises, a tax shelter.

"If you don't think I'm being presumptuous—" She hesitated, trying to find the right kind of face to go with her offer. "If you don't think it's too outrageous of me." She slipped on her horn-rims and pulled open a desk drawer. "Let me advance you the money, and we shan't say a word to *him*."

She wrote out a check on her own account at Barclay's Bank for fifteen hundred francs.

Eleven

He kept the cab waiting while he packed. He carried a trench coat over one arm—the Burberry he hoped made him look like a foreign correspondent instead of a travel-guide writer—and tossed a packet of flat toilet tissue into the open suit-case (you never knew in Europe, not even in Switzerland). There was a reassuring leather-covered quarter-liter flask of vodka tucked among his socks and undershorts.

He had the feeling time pressed, but the train did not

leave until that evening. The thought of a trip happily distracted him—though he had temporarily forgotten where he was going and why: his injured sense of justice (J-P was his son as much as hers) was suspended for the moment. For now he was simply glad of the train ticket in his trench coat pocket, the new bank notes in his billfold.

As he stepped out the side door he saw the old women crossing from their side of the terrace, alternating patterns of sun and shade on their broken straw hats as they walked under the trellis of dead vines. Whenever they walked together like that, in perfect step, he saw their names up in lights—THE MAZARIN SISTERS—and half expected them to raise their canes in unison and shuffle into an antique vaudeville routine.

They always wore black, in mourning for the men they never had—there must be a legion of these women without men. (There was a legion of men without women, too, like Grimwald, like himself.) One sister was half deaf, the other half blind: this was the only way he could tell Mademoiselle Bérénice from Mademoiselle Béatrice, for they dressed and looked alike, wore interchangeable aprons and carpet slippers and towels across their shoulders for shawls. The patches on their aprons were stitched and double-stitched and re-patched over so many worn-away years that the overlay was as rich and thick as armor plate. You would not know they were well-to-do—perhaps they did not know it themselves (they were drifting into senility) because of the constant games of subterfuge they played with the tax collector. They asked Paul to pay the rent in cash, suspicious of the fiscal trail a check left, and Paul had seen them tuck that very cash into the soiled linen of their laundry basket.

They were talking together in the Italianate Niçoise patios

until they saw Paul, and cried out: *"Pour le petit!"* as one sister raised high the paper sack she was carrying. A gift for the little one—but how did they know he was on his way to see his son? Then he remembered the post card from Leysin this morning: one of the sisters was illiterate, but the other was not.

The sack was full of lemons from the lemon tree under Paul's window.

He had purposely left the sack of lemons in the cab, but as soon as he got out at the station, the driver called after him: *"Votre sac, monsieur!"* Paul accepted the lemons with a rueful smile and muttered, *"Merci."*

When the Lyon-Genève train pulled into the station Paul abandoned the sack of lemons on a bench in the second-class waiting room. He had reserved space in the second-class couchettes (dreading the ordeal: passengers stacked three high on two sides of an airless compartment—airless, because the French have this thing about drafts), but his compartment was empty except for a young boy and his girl, Americans (U.S. flags sewn to the flaps of their backpacks), so he took the opportunity to ease the compartment window open an inch for air and was about to pull down the shade to hide the opening when he heard someone shouting from the quay. He opened the window wider. An old man was shouting at him, waving frantically as the train began to move. Then the man began to jog alongside the train, his face growing flushed under his white hair; Paul feared he would have a heart attack. Someone in the crowd caught up the cry, *"Monsieur!"* and snatched the sack from the old man, then tossed it to another man nearer the train. At last the lemons were held aloft and passed through the window to Paul. After he saluted the old man and called out "*Merci!*" he put the lemons in his suitcase, convinced finally they were meant to go with him to Switzerland.

Paul decided to assume the identity of René de Cygne, in case the Americans attempted to include him in the conversation. But he did not have to play that game. They must have thought he was French from his cheap briefcase.

The girl said, "At least there's only him so far," assuming he would not understand English.

"*Je m'excuse,*" murmured Paul, and climbed into the top berth to give them stretching space to prop their long legs across the back packs stashed in the aisle. They gave him a sullen glance, then ignored him. Good. They spoke no French. Nothing worse than Americans in France who knew French, because that was the only thing they knew. The boy opened a bottle of wine, drank from it first, then passed it to the girl.

Paul lay on his back with his arms up, head in his hands, listening to the wine sloshing back and forth. An occasional phrase drifted up from below.

"Siena was a riot."

"Rome's O.K. but Verona's a drag."

Paul assumed they had been together all through Italy, but now he realized they had only just met. How easily travelers fall in together, how quickly they form touring parties according to nationality and age.

"I was getting only six hundred liras to the dollar in Venice."

"In Rome I was getting seven-fifty, but I knew this black-market guy that hung around the Spanish Steps."

They both wore hard-traveling jeans; their hair was the same shoulder length, their voices incredibly alike. Paul could hardly distinguish his voice from hers.

"When you going back?"

"When I run out of money."

The wine reminded Paul he had a nightcap of his own; he took the flask of vodka from the suitcase. He sipped at it, listening to the familiar flat speech, but foreign too, watching the Riviera lights float past the window.

At Toulon they were joined by an Old Testament Jew wearing a beret instead of a skull cap. He closed the compartment window before he struggled into the middle bunk.

Long after Paul had switched off his reading lamp he heard the two Americans crowd together into his—or her—narrow berth.

"Where am I supposed to put my elbow?"

"Hey, that tickles."

He wondered what the ancient Jew thought—if he was awake and heard. Paul did not know if it was the boy or girl who murmured: "Yeah, do that. Nice, ah. I like it."

Paul had met Sylvie on a cruise ship in the Mediterranean (and he had never really left the Mediterranean shore since). In seven days at sea he had never once managed to maneuver the pretty Swiss passenger to the romantic afterdeck railing —no matter how tranquil the water and starlit the night sky. Sylvie had always slipped away from the shadows and steered them both toward the light. Afterward, when they were married, she confessed she was afraid of him on the ship. Just before the cruise she had read in *France-Soir* of a shipboard murder, a girl strangled in the dark and tossed overboard by her lover.

But he had courted her in the ship's bar drinking Campari and soda and had kissed her, the first time, in the smoky, paneled midship salon: her kisses were cool and sweet and simply given. They once kissed across a candle in a café in

Genoa (one of the sight-seeing stops on the cruise), and the shoulder pad of Paul's jacket caught fire. She threw wine on the smoldering burn, then drew back aghast—but Paul was laughing so hard she finally had to laugh too.

Her first gift to him was a copy of *French Without Toil*, and she began to teach him to speak correctly: a crisp, diligent, hard-driving European teacher. He put up with the lessons simply to be with her—the only verb he wanted to conjugate was *aimer*.

It was amusing to watch the queer lip movements she used to form the vowel sounds, o's and u's he would never in a lifetime learn to pronounce. (Frenchmen, he realized, have a peculiarly mobile upper lip; even his son had it, from speaking French.) How could Americans stand hearing their language spoken with an accent? she asked him. They love it, he told her, especially a French accent.

She was pedantic about her own faults in English and insisted he correct her grammar and pronunciation; she had the gift of languages and pushed herself toward perfection. But he was so delighted by her quaint "hind of the ship" (and "tempest" and "serpent") he could not bring himself to correct her.

The voices from below broke into his reverie:

"Try it."

"I don't want to."

They spoke softly now, and Paul strained to hear which one said what.

"Not that way. I never did it."

"You're hung up on sanitation. Just try it."

"The whole idea turns me off. I mean it."

"Like this. Just taste it."

"I don't want to."

"Come on."

"I'm afraid to throw up."

How innocent we were, thought Paul. He had met Sylvie in a time of ships and candles and *French Without Toil*, a decade ago, an age only Paul remembered.

Twelve

"*Quelle surprise*," she said, showing no surprise at all. Somehow Madame Chaix seemed to block his way to Sylvie, sitting in the lobby between Paul and the elevator.

He fumbled the ritual kiss when she turned the very cheek he was aiming for, their heads bobbing apart like chickens. When he did kiss each sagging downy cheek in turn, he asked himself: Is this what my wife will be in thirty years? His mother-in-law had a Cinzano on the low table near at hand, and her knitting in her lap.

"Where's Sylvie?"

"*Comment?*"

"Where's Sylvie?"

"Ah, Sylvie. As she did not expect you, she is skiing."

"And Jean-Paul?"

"*Comment?*"

He sometimes wondered if her deafness was not just a way to evade him, to ignore him or to make him out a fool. She had no difficulty understanding the words Sylvie spoke.

"And Jean-Paul?"

"Also. He skis with the Miniclub, on the Little Slope. They will return for lunch. Will you have an apéritif?"

At times he could not believe his mother-in-law was the enemy she appeared to be; he might have been wrong about her from the beginning. This small dry creature (but with nerves of piano wire) had her own solitude to deal with; trying to fill an empty life, she reached out the way any mother would. Her modest wealth was the eternal barrier between them; Paul saw himself the way she must have looked at him: an interloper from a different world who could not provide a living for his wife and son. She was not the villain of his dilemma. He realized she was no more than a benign adversary, a self-satisfied woman growing old. She turned a deaf ear to her son-in-law at the same time she offered him a drink.

But as badly as Paul needed a drink, he did not intend to linger at his mother-in-law's elbow, accepting her largesse. (She wore a necklace of those interlocking plastic tokens around her neck: the only form of currency the club bar would accept.) He thanked her but excused himself—he would look for his family on the slopes. She offered to guard his suitcase; she placed her drink on it, to assure him it was safe with her.

Paul headed for the sugar-coated hillside crisscrossed with ski tracks. He followed a trail of blood—nosebleed?—leading to an agonized Christ in a birdhouse perched on a fence-post, a station of the cross. At a house that had once been a tuberculosis clinic he paused to read a plaque: *Dans cette maison le docteur Auguste Rollier a conçu des 1903 et mis au point* . . . the good doctor had invented heliotherapy for the treatment of tuberculosis. Why am I reading this? Paul asked himself. Another piece of useless information I can pass on to my son.

He stood there, stalling, out of his element—the snow, the altitude—angry at himself, miserable. He was in no hurry to meet his wife.

He sneezed. The Burberry was too light, the low-cut Italian shoes too thin for winter country. Heliotherapy would help—or a pair of boots like Miss Bishop's. Perhaps Madame Chaix would knit him a scarf. His wife's mother thought him a fool. So did his wife. Nevertheless, he said to himself (a little high on the rarefied air), I am trustworthy, loyal, helpful, friendly—

He came across ELZA EN LOUIS spelled out in stones against a snowbank, framed in a Valentine heart. Paul sneezed again, this time into the heart of ELZA EN LOUIS.

He passed a patisserie window full of glazed pastry and went in to buy a Napoleon for J-P. When he came out he realized J-P could not eat pastry. He began eating it himself, overjoyed to discover it had been soaked in rum.

The closer he came to the blurred figures circling down-hill along the white face of the mountain and dangling from ski lifts like a strung-out line of washing, the larger his panic grew. He should never have come. The back of his throat was painfully constricted: the beginning of a cold, or the sour taste of his mistake—and now it was too late. He walked ankle deep in mud-stained snow till he came to a quaint series of fossilized cow droppings and—as J-P might have done—used them as stepping stones. The dour Swiss faces at the edge of the crowd of spectators turned from the skiers to watch this idiot dancing from turd to turd.

Just beyond the parked cars was a line of children hustled into position by monitors, tags around their necks for the lift—which child was his own? The tags reminded Paul of those D.P. tags Europeans wore at refugee centers: the Western world of fathers and sons separated by war, bombed to a pulp if they fled in the wrong direction. His heart was hurting. He was a displaced person himself.

"Papa, Papa! I know how to make a *chasse-neige!*"

J-P, in his red-white-and-blue anorak, was skiing toward him. Paul pushed through an opening between the bundles of hay used as a backstop; he hurried toward the *piste* and opened his arms, reaching for his son, when he felt a spray of snow as if from a snow plow to his left. A skier slammed into him from that side, grunting, "No, no!" toppled him and plunged them both into a wet white snowdrift; skis, arms, and legs entangled, her goggles dislodged and her hair unwound from beneath the wool cap: Sylvie. He should have recognized her from her scent.

"Why are you *here?*" Sylvie was up in an instant, her ski poles pulled from under his armpits. "Where did you *come* from?"

J-P wept behind his fogged goggles, crying: *"Papa est blessé"* and sure enough, a spasm of pain shot through Paul's back when he tried to lift himself.

Two monitors with red-cross emblems on their sleeves skied up beside Paul and unrolled the canvas stretcher they carried between them. Paul was quickly, deftly maneuvered onto the stretcher and transported on skis to a rickety aid station barricaded behind bales of hay. J-P and Sylvie skied not far behind the stretcher bearers; when they pulled up beside the stretcher and Paul looked into Sylvie's face upside down, he wondered if her skin was chapped or was it rage that turned it red.

The doctor was looking at his wristwatch when Paul was brought in: he did not look up. The clinic smelled of ether and wool socks drying on a radiator, but for all the rustic interior, Paul was reassured to note an x-ray screen and one wall lined with cylinders of oxygen. There was even a television set, turned on, but the screen projecting nothing but a blur of flickering white streaks, like a snowstorm. The only other bed was occupied by a man with an oxygen mask attached to the lower part of his face.

"L'altitude," announced the doctor—to himself, to the

stretcher bearers, to anyone who cared to hear—"*est très mauvais pour le coeur.*"

"What were you *doing* out there?" asked Sylvie, anguished.

She did not expect an answer to this, so Paul offered none. J-P had got out of his skis and was worriedly chewing the edge of his ski-lift tag. From time to time he cast a frightened look in the direction of the man with the oxygen mask.

"*Vous avez de l'assurance?*" asked one of the monitors, and Paul was reminded of an American hospital admittance desk asking for Blue Cross or bank reference.

Sylvie fumbled in her anorak pocket for documents.

"But for *monsieur*," said the attendant.

"*Il est mon mari.*"

The word "husband," even in French, sounded peculiar in Sylvie's mouth. Perhaps by breaking his back Paul had reestablished conjugal status.

The attendants were speaking German together, looking at Sylvie's insurance papers. The doctor joined them.

"Insured?"

"I have the FSS Insurance."

"But the injured man?"

"He's my husband."

"I'm her husband," said Paul.

"That has no bearing," said the doctor. "*Monsieur* must be insured as well."

"But I am insured for anyone I injure," insisted Sylvie.

The doctor checked the document again—he had not yet checked the patient—and shook his head, negative: "You are not. You have not the omnium policy which covers all. You have yourself and child insured. You are insured also against damages the victim might seek if a *procès* is undertaken."

"I'm not going to sue," said Paul.

"Please," Sylvie said to him, "don't say anything."

"But what's all this about insurance? I could be lying here with a backlash, or whatever they call it."

Instead of returning the insurance document to Sylvie, the doctor passed it to one of the attendants, asking, "Is it not so?"

"I wasn't even skiing," said Paul.

"Not skiing?" The doctor reached for the document again. A stretcher bearer confirmed that Paul was not on skis when the accident occurred. The language was French again.

"I don't even know how to ski," said Paul.

Sylvie's face seemed to crease down the middle: "Let me talk, please."

"Then there is no question," said the doctor, "*pas question.*" He rubbed his pink white hands together, washing them of the whole affair. "*Monsieur* was on the *piste* illegally and thus is uncovered by accidental insurance of any kind."

When the doctor walked away to check on his heart patient, Paul called after him: "What about my back?"

"I will inspect your back presently."

Sylvie was staring fixedly—angrily, Paul assumed—into the television snowstorm. But she did, he reflected, carry his trenchcoat draped over one arm, *noblesse oblige.* Paul desperately wanted a cigarette out of the coat pocket, but there was a sign posted above the cylinders of oxygen: NO SMOKING, in four languages.

In a short while the doctor did return to Paul, strip away his shirt and explore his spine, ribs and lower back. His touch was sure, gentle even. If only Sylvie would touch him like that—if only Sylvie would touch him.

"A sprain, I would judge," announced the doctor, "but we will see what the *radio* tells us."

The radio meant x-ray, and the two stretcher bearers eased Paul onto a revolving stool (he felt the old spasm again) and propped him up stiffly behind the screen.

"Take a deep breath, hold it."

The gadget reminded Paul of those automatic photo machines in train stations, three snapshots for one franc. A light came on, and the doctor squinted into it, his face oddly lighted from below. J-P came around to look, to see inside his father, chewing away a corner of his ski-lift tag. Sylvie did not join the witnesses. Just as well, thought Paul, in case I turn out to be hollow.

"Nothing." The light went off. "A sprain only. Rest in bed. Heat applied to the back will help. You will be fine, my friend, in a day or two."

I will never be fine again, thought Paul, and I am not your friend. He could not help thinking the diagnosis would have been more serious if he were covered by insurance.

There was the sound of a siren in the distance, and the doctor said, "Ah, they are coming." For the heart patient, no doubt. The doctor went to the man and put an ear to his chest; Paul could see the eyes above the oxygen mask, large and full of pain.

As the ambulance came nearer the sound seemed to fill the small clinic. Sylvie turned to Paul; her ordinarily immaculate hair had come loose from the coiled braid. She stared through him to a place beyond them both: the piercing, frantic wail of the siren might have been a scream inside her trying to get out. J-P put his hands over his ears, but by then the ambulance was at the door and the sound went down to a sputtering whine.

The ambulance driver held open the door for the stretcher bearers who had taken up the heart patient, oxygen and all, and carried him outside. Sylvie turned to watch. "It is a region," said the doctor, "not recommended for the heart."

In the grim silence that followed, it was Paul, not Sylvie, who exploded. "Do you hear what he said?" he shouted at Sylvie's back, as if with his pronouncement the doctor had sealed their fate.

Thirteen

Complet placards hung like holiday wreaths from every hotel door in Leysin—no room at any inn—but Paul, riding the euphoric shot the doctor gave him, did not give a dreamy damn, so they drove in snowy figure eights with Joan Duff in the taxi (yes, Joan, out of thin air, out of *rarefied* air, Duff's wife; he had not seen her since Amazing Growth went under, since Duff disappeared). Joan was also at the Hôtel des Voyageurs, also *complet* (unthinkable a man should sleep with his own wife; his own wife slept with her mother), for Joan, in her own words, had bird-dogged Duff here and she intended to bloodhound him to death now that she'd tracked him down (amazing to think of Duff of Amazing Growth at this altitude). "Only forty kilometers from here," said Joan, "straight up," and the finger she pointed out the cab window was her middle finger. They made a hopeless run from hotel to hotel to find an inn to put Paul in.

"All you think about is what you want, when you want it, and that's why—"

"I wanted to see J-P."

"*Tu ne penses qu'à toi-même.* Yourself first. Like the chocolate egg Maman sent Jean-Paul last Easter."

"What egg?"

"That my mother sent. To Jean-Paul. For Easter."

"Your mother has a brutal mouth."

"Jesus," said Joan, with a giggle at the back of her throat. "What'd you say he got in that injection?"

"My mother has what?"

"A mouth like a shark."

"Don't speak of my mother. My mother sent Jean-Paul an Easter egg and you ate it."

"What egg?"

"I cannot eat chocolate," said J-P.

"That's right," said Paul, "he can't even eat chocolate."

"You didn't have to eat it."

"Jesus," said Joan, "you guys are amateurs at this. Duff and I used to slug it out with baseball bats."

They came to a hotel perched on the edge of an abyss, *complet*. Then the driver remembered a pension where there might be a vacancy, called the Cinq Etoiles.

"Only five?" asked Paul.

"What I'd like to have," said Joan, "is some of whatever that doctor gave Paul."

By the time they got to the Cinq Etoiles, Sylvie had withdrawn into her corner; she would not get out of the cab. The vacant room was on the third floor of a three-story chalet with an outside staircase. All of Leysin was *complet*, the porter informed them—this was the only room in town.

"I'll take it," said Paul. "I'm collecting the last of everything."

"*Comment?*"

"He's had an injection," Joan explained.

The porter went on to say the former occupant had been taken to the hospital only that day, the victim of a heart attack while skiing.

"I know," said Paul. "I met him."

Joan and the taxi driver helped Paul up the slippery outside staircase to a tiny garret room under the eaves. Joan took off his shoes and got him into bed under the thick duvet.

"Look, we're next-door neighbors," said Joan.

There was a view of the roof of the Hôtel des Voyageurs.

"You can have the place," said Paul. "I wouldn't stay at a hotel that took plastic beads at the bar instead of money."

"Oh boy, are you high."

"Only three storys."

"You're looped, and I love it."

"I'm the last of something, and I collect the last of everything."

He was not sure he had been kissed till he saw the lipstick print between his eyes, in the armoire mirror opposite the bed. It was not Sylvie's kiss by proxy—it was just Joan's. The injection was wearing off, and she left him to lick his wounds, to brood alone under the solid pine beam that bisected the ceiling, a beam a man could count on, could confidently hang himself from if he were desperate enough and could get out from under his leaden duvet to climb a chair.

The evening of the third day at the Cinq Etoiles, Paul sat in a straight-backed chair at the window (his back injury little more than a stiff memory of a bad time) enjoying a Swiss cigarette and watching the snow turn red on the roof of the Hôtel des Voyageurs. He wondered which of the hundred windows was hers, and what she was doing at this moment—drinking an apéritif, no doubt, with Maman. He had not seen his wife since that ill-fated first day. Madame Chaix had sent his suitcase to him, and a novel by Agatha Christie in French. J-P came by between ski lessons to chatter about the chamois he saw on the slopes and ask if owls (he pronounced *olls*) ate mice dead or alive and play cards with Papa. He had received a game from his grandmother called

Champignons, an educational game that taught the players how to identify edible and poisonous mushrooms. Too tame, Paul told J-P. He was teaching his son to play poker.

So far, today, Paul had spoken to no one but the bovine chambermaid who brought up his meals. The spartan room lacked a telephone, or he might have called someone, anyone, just to hear a human voice. He would have called Sylvie just to hear her say *Allo,* breathed heavily, then hung up.

There was a centimeter of vodka in the flask; Paul drained it quickly, as if to get it over with. Maybe he could send the maid somewhere for a bottle. Among its other failings, the Cinq Etoiles had no liquor license.

Something moved through the snowy passageway between hotels. An unidentified flying object, maybe—no, it was earthbound, making tracks in the snow. Paul's blood stirred, his scalp tingled. He waited for the familiar effect: all sound muted, his ear in a seashell—the little girl, an Alpine version of her, was about to appear.

What would he say to her the first time they spoke together? She would be his daughter, if he had a daughter. He allowed the vision to take possession of him—it was better than a drink. She was only a shadow against the snow, but a shadow that left footprints. Don't sweat it. If he tried to make sense of the apparition there would be a big nothing again. Let it be. She was his daughter, her name was Christine.

He tried to reassemble last night's nightmare, a dream he had intended to doctor (and cut) and tell J-P as a bedtime story. He would tell it to Christine. Would a shrewd little ghost coming out of the void fall for a secondhand tale? Once upon a time. Should he tell it in English or French? Once upon a time, *il était une fois.* No, English—this was a true-blue daughter of the U.S.A. Once upon a time a king (make him a king, he was a fool in the original) was trapped in a tower of ice. Right, and he was held there under an evil spell—no fault of his own. (She was sure to ask who cast the spell in the first place.) A witch, of course. Why? asked the little girl. A good question: it's the nature of witches to cast spells, evil or otherwise; wicked witch of the east or wicked witch of the west, no matter which, they were all alike in that. Anyway, the king had to find a way out of his refrigerated prison before sundown or his son, the prince (make it a daughter, the princess) would freeze to death in the snowdrifts outside. (This has to have a happy ending, Paul told himself.) But it had no ending at all. By then Paul recognized the phantom visitor's long-legged stride: it was Joan Duff, in her Christmas sable, approaching the outside staircase.

In a moment Joan let herself in (without knocking) and tossed a cigar box and a hot-water bottle on the bed. She quickly shed the fur.

"A message," she said breathlessly, "from your ever-loving wife."

In a hot-water bottle? Even a castaway on a desert isle had better luck. But Paul was hopeful in spite of all.

"What message?"

"Not exactly 'Happy New Year,' honey."

"What exactly, then?"

"They're checking out. She's taking J-P home. He's a cute kid, your son. He calls me Tante Joan."

Paul flicked his cigarette out the window in the direction of the Hôtel des Voyageurs.

"She sent you the hot-water bottle for your back."

"Thanks. My back's O.K. now." His back, suddenly, hurt as much as ever.

"Full of hot water, no less. I asked her, 'Are you kidding?' "

"Sylvie never kids."

"She said you've got no hot water over here."

"She's right." Paul wished Joan would put her fur back on and go.

"Anyway, I poured the water out and filled the thing full of rum."

"Great, thanks. I can get all the hot water I want, the chambermaid brings it up in a pitcher. But rum I could use." He held his flask upside down to show how empty it was.

Joan took this as an invitation to stay. She planted herself on Paul's bed with her legs crossed at her après-ski boots, arms bent backwards supporting her hunched shoulders, her pert little breasts thrust out at the world in general, at Paul in particular.

He should have kept the outside door locked and pretended to be René de Cygne.

Joan, Sylvie always said, was a typical American. How would Sylvie know? The only American she knew was Paul. Joan was from California, which made her typical of something. She was pretty enough in repose, but she was seldom in repose and she was an obsessive conversationalist. She had lovely hands (if hands counted for anything), and she knew it. She was forever gesturing and she wore enough bracelets so that if her hands did not catch your attention her bracelets would. Before she married Duff she modeled wristwatches in Geneva.

As much as he wanted solace and needed company, Paul felt uncomfortable with Joan Duff in the room. Feline muscles rippled under her dress whenever she changed position: her vibes were stronger than his, her scent disturbingly unfamiliar. She fixed him in her relentless gaze with those slightly protuberant eyes of hers, the brown irises swimming in white (she seemed never to blink), that look of perpetual astonishment—though Paul could think of nothing that would astonish Joan. But he was wrong.

"You want to know something?" (No, thought Paul.) "Duff and I always figured you and Sylvie were the married king and queen of the world."

Paul pictured himself as a chess piece. The queen was the most powerful player on the board, the king was a weakling.

"All the time I was with that bastard I kept wishing our marriage could be like yours."

Paul lighted another cigarette.

"What the hell," said Joan, "nobody gets married any more."

"Yes they do," said Paul.

"Or stays married, if they're dumb enough to try."

"Yes they do."

"Marriage is for the birds, honey. It's a dead end, this day and age."

"I don't know."

"Listen, what people ought to do, people ought to meet and ball each other and just say *merci* or *danke* or *mille grazie* on the way out."

"That's what people do."

"But it ought to be official. And they should at least say thanks."

"How do you like your rum?" asked Paul, to change the subject.

"With Coke. We can see the old year out with rum Cokes."

"Not only is there no hot water in this establishment, there's no Coca-Cola either. Is this New Year's Eve?"

"Didn't you know?"

"We live very quietly here. You mean Sylvie's leaving tonight?"

"Your wife is in bed, where all good girls ought to be. She checks out tomorrow morning at dawn."

"Did she, by any chance—"

"No, she didn't. Relax. She sent you her hot-water bottle —what more do you want?" Joan picked up the hot-water bottle and dropped it in Paul's lap on her way to the window. "No Coca-Cola. O.K., but don't tell me there's no ice. If there's one thing Switzerland's got, it's ice."

"She could have at least sent me a note."

"Don't sweat it. I never saw a guy so hung up on his wife. Marriage, I'm telling you, is for the birds. Everybody's marriage cracks sooner or later—so what's the big deal?"

"It's not cracked. It's just a trial separation."

"Don't make me laugh."

Joan pushed the window open, and Paul exhaled a cloud of smoke, then inhaled a breath of frosted air so sharp it made his chest ache. Outside it was growing dark. He felt giddy, faint. He caught himself studying the sharply outlined panties under Joan's dress as she leaned far forward and almost left the ground. She had nice hollows, he realized, at the backs of her knees where her legs sprouted out of the long-haired boots.

Joan was giggling when she came back inside: the icicle she had broken from the overhanging roof was shaped like a frozen phallus.

"I've only got one glass, and it's plastic."

Joan chucked the penis of ice into Paul's toothbrush glass; Paul poured from the hot-water bottle. They took a ritual sip each.

"It tastes tinny," said Joan.

"From the roof. I've got some lemons in my suitcase, but don't ask me how they got there."

"Beautiful, beautiful." (Duff used to say that.) "We can make daiquiris!" Joan had sugar cubes in her purse: Sylvie had given her a supply when she took J-P for a haircut, in case of malaise. She flipped open Paul's suitcase, saying, "Lemons, lemons. Never come to Switzerland without your lemons." Suddenly she turned sad, and said, "Is this all you've got in the world? Your socks aren't even silk. All Duff's socks were silk."

Joan sliced the lemons on the rim of the wash basin with her vicious-looking nail file. She added the lemon juice and sugar cubes to the rum. Paul watched uneasily, unhappy with the way Joan (slowly, looking up at him with her mock-astonished eyes) inserted the phallic tube of ice into the narrow rubberoid opening of the hot-water bottle.

"I think you have to break the ice up," said Paul.

"You break me up."

She smashed the ice in the basin with the bottom of a brass ashtray. When Joan shook the hot-water bottle, bartender style, Paul realized she was not wearing a brassière.

"Not so tinny this time," said Joan, sipping.

"A little rubbery, maybe."

"It's good, actually."

"It's a drink. Happy New Year."

"Don't say it yet!" shrieked Joan. "It's bad luck. Don't say it until midnight."

"By midnight I expect to be, like all good boys, asleep."

Not long before midnight they were still trading anecdotes about Duff, passing the toothbrush glass back and forth like sophomores sharing a joint. Joan pulled some clippings out of her purse, from *l'Express* and *Der Spiegel*, about the House that Duff Built, and the offshore swindle of the century ("The Incredible Decline of Amazing Growth," as *Newsweek* put it). Paul had read the item in *l'Express* months ago and he did not read German, so Joan carefully—even proudly, he thought—folded the clippings into her purse again.

"He's out of his mind. Calls himself King of the Drop-outs and won't let anybody in."

"Then why do you want me to go see him?"

"You he'll see. He likes you, he always did. I know he's got some screwy deal going—maybe there's something in it for you."

"I don't know."

"Call him, he'll invite you up. It's like a monastery where he's hiding out, it used to be a T.B. sanitarium—Duff must be crawling the walls by now. But I can't get near the bastard. There's a nun up there with orders to shoot me on sight."

"Do you think he might want to buy up some securities?"

"What securities?"

Paul had naïvely believed his own publicity and—without consulting Duff (or telling Sylvie)—had sunk more than seven thousand dollars in A.G. stock and bearer bonds.

"Amazing Growth."

"Don't make me laugh."

"I thought he might be planning a comeback or something. Buy up stocks and corner the market."

"Don't make me laugh, honey—there ain't no market. A.G. is dead and Duff's the one that killed it."

"I just thought."

"Your stock?"

"No," he lied. He did not want to make her laugh.

"Go up and see him," said Joan, "he likes you. But don't trust the bastard any farther than you can toss a grand piano."

The makeshift daiquiris had begun to turn his stomach: he sat stiffly in the straight-backed chair tasting a mixture of heartburn and regret. Still, Joan might be right. Wherever Duff was, there was bound to be money; and Paul was broke and going nowhere with Grimwald. He likes me, Paul assured himself. If Duff had hitched his wagon to another star, maybe he could tag along, just for the ride, before the star burned itself out.

"I don't know," said Joan, looking wistful, sad, "in some ways I still love the bastard."

Why not? thought Paul. He had been asking himself *why not?* all night.

"He was the one person that could always make me laugh."

She had even brought along a box of cigars she wanted Paul to give the bastard.

"You want to know something Duff said about you?" (No, thought Paul.) "He said he'd swear you never slept with anybody but your wife."

"Tell him to tell Sylvie that—it might help."

"Is it true?"

"You mean, from the time I married Sylvie or before?"

"After, silly."

"Yes," he confessed, and he was not sure why he was annoyed with himself for saying it. "I'm the last of the squares."

"I don't care if you're the original—but shit, why so pure? Do you think Miss Switzerland would pass up a chance at a romp if the right stud came along?"

He would have to think about that. He thought about it for an instant and said, "Not Sylvie."

"I could tell you something about women, but I won't. I don't want to spoil anybody's starry-eyed notions of us. I think it's sweet."

He listened for the sarcasm in her voice.

"I really do." She looked wistfully at the hot-water bottle in her lap. "The swingers, love, will not inherit the earth. But Christ, Duff could be funny sometimes."

She always talked about Duff in the past tense, as if he had died.

"You want to know something the bastard did one time?" (No, thought Paul.) "It was when we were living in Geneva and he came home one night and said, 'I did it, honey.' He said he had got himself a vasectomy. 'A vasectomy?' I said. That's what he said. He said it only took about fifteen minutes, right there in the doctor's office, and he showed me— you know Duff—just dropped his pants and there it was all bandaged up, even his balls. He couldn't wait to try it out, even though the doctor said you had to wait a week. 'Are you out of your mind?' I said. 'It might tear open,' I told him, 'or bleed or something.' But he insisted it was stitched tight as a sausage and nothing could happen, so how about it? Right then and there. Then the idiot unwrapped it to show me. I was all eyes, I admit. I was fascinated, in fact, in a horrible kind of way. But it was nothing. I mean there was nothing there—just Duff's same old dangle dangling out— no scar, no nothing. He invented the whole stunt, the bastard, and put the bandages on himself, to set me up." Joan dabbed at her moist eyes with the backs of her wrists, as if she had laughed herself tearful. "I mean, Duff in those days was the living end."

"I can't," said Paul. "My back."
"I'll give you a back rub."

"Give me another drink instead."

"Sorry," she was shaking the empty hot-water bottle, and her breasts. "All out."

Joan was pretending to be drunker than she was, and Paul was pretending to be sober. She took a coin out of her purse and put it into the slot at the bed's headboard to show Paul how the built-in vibrator worked. Then she pulled off her après-ski boots and padded over to Paul to peck at his shirt buttons.

"No hot water," said Paul, "but I've got a bed with an automatic massager."

"That's the Swiss for you. If there was a way to put a meter on a faucet you'd have had hot water. Come over here."

Since it was no longer a question of friendship, the boss's wife, puritan virtue, loyalty to Sylvie—why not? The standards you bring from Cincinnati to France do not herein apply.

She was humming "What Are You Doing New Year's Eve" as he watched her pull up her sweater and step out of her skirt—like watching a child undress for bed. How could she wear wool against her naked skin? She seemed whiter than Sylvie, maybe because of the contrast: Joan's darker triangle of hair. She left her pantyhose in a little ball of gauze on the floor.

"First I'm going to give you an alcoholic rub."

"What's that?"

"That's a rub an alcoholic gives."

They got into the quivering bed together, on top of the duvet, Paul face down. She straddled him. "There," she said, motherly, and began to rub his back and shoulders with her wristwatch-model hands.

"Nice," said Paul. It was hard to breathe with his face buried in a mound of duvet feathers.

"Didn't I tell you?" She unfastened his belt and lowered his pants. "Now turn yourself over."

Why not? He turned, thinking about the young lovers in the train. People ought to meet and ball each other, as easy as that, thought Paul, growing hard easily.

"Just leave it to Joannie," said Joan. "I got a feeling they've neglected the hell out of you." She addressed herself, not to Paul, but to his rising penis.

They joined. Joan was large and liquid. Looking up at her, at the dimpled moons of her breasts and flaring nostrils, Paul felt himself go soft. It would be ridiculous if he could not perform—maybe just as ridiculous if he could. He closed his eyes, gritted his teeth and grew hard again. With his eyes closed he could imagine Sylvie had mounted him, though Sylvie would never have assumed that position.

"Hey, I like it up here. Duff, naturally, never let anybody get on top of him."

Paul kept his eyes closed and hoped Joan would stop talking. As long as he did not see her or hear her voice he could fix the flickering image of Sylvie in his mind.

"Wait a minute," croaked Joan hoarsely, and he felt her pull off. Damn, she was fumbling in her purse—for her diaphragm, Paul assumed, but no. She put another Swiss franc in the slot to keep the bed vibrating.

When they resumed he was soft again: the duvet, though it quivered under him, was no magic feather cloud going anywhere. And it was hard to imagine Sylvie riding him from above—he had trouble picturing her legs folded jockey style at his sides. But Joan was there with her California savoir-faire to lead him on, so he closed his eyes and ground his teeth and worked at it until he was hard. As long as the bed joggled him and Joan manipulated him, it was easy. Not Joan, he reminded himself, but Sylvie. Sylvie, urgent for once, moving hard against him with little falling gasps of pleasure—until the long drawn-out final moan that faded to a sigh. It was easy. And Paul was so delighted to have provoked her pleasure he immediately came to his own spurting release.

Still joined, relaxed, Joan wanted to talk. Paul shut her out and listened for Sylvie. He heard a sound from next door, a shout muffled by snow—then whistles, a firecracker, music, applause.

"Happy New Year, lover." She kissed him with her tongue.

"Sounds wild next door. Sounds like you missed the gala soirée."

"No I didn't," said Joan.

For more than an hour he had needed to urinate, lying there till the day broke mistily through the mountain crests. Joan lay curled against him, tightly attached to him, a squid holding its prey. She was snoring. He finally eased himself out from under her tentacles; he slipped out of bed and stood upright, one leg numb. He limped across the room in the half light on his way to the beautiful enamel Swiss chamber pot tucked under the chair. God bless the Swiss— they do, like the Parisians, provide a man a place to piss.

Naked, he shivered in the drafty room, his bare feet on the cold pine boards. He put a towel over his shoulders in imitation of a Mazarin sister and went to the window to close it. Then, through the granulated windowpanes he watched a circle of crows cawing over the garbage cans behind the Hôtel des Voyageurs. One window was still lighted —or already lighted—and he wondered if it was hers. He wanted to shout his love across the narrow chasm between them, but, with his luck, feared the words would bring down an avalanche.

Fourteen

He was in poor shape for a fool's errand. As he went up in the *crémaillère* his Cinq Etoiles breakfast would not go down—something to do with gravity, thought he, or the daiquiris he drank with Joan. At fifteen hundred meters his pen began to leak and his nose was running. He dared not look back at the Swiss village falling away below: cable cars made Paul's head spin.

The desk clerk at the Hôtel des Volageurs had confirmed the news: yes, Madame Chaix and Madame Swanson and *le petit garçon* had left early this morning. Paul used the hotel telephone (since the Cinq Etoiles had none), wondering if Duff would be up at noon on New Year's Day. It was not Duff who answered: a sharp voice (a woman?—the connection was poor) informed him Monsieur Duff would return his call within thirty minutes. Paul would have to wait in the hotel lobby until Duff called him back—but where else could he go? (Joan had said goodbye already, then *merci, danke* and *mille grazie*.) He gave the number of the Hôtel des Voyageurs.

While waiting for the call, Paul sat in the glass booth with the door open watching a corps of waiters set up buffet tables at the entrance to the dining room. Piecemeal, in tray-laden relays, they built up a patchwork sculpture of cold lobster, langoustes, shelled oysters and rosy crevettes arranged symmetrically against a beachhead of blue ice. There were bottles of Riesling and *vin rosé* imbedded in ice buckets, and a vast display of sliced ham, cold roast beef and paper-thin filets d'Anvers with a salver of caviar as a centerpiece. The *salade Niçoise* created a baroque effect; Paul thought he recognized the professional style and wondered idly if the salad chef had studied with a Parisian he once interviewed. Something very *pompes funèbres* about the arrangement: wreaths of celery, bouquets of chilled cauliflower, radishes carved into rosettes. A ruffled frame of lettuce made a crepelike lining to the silver coffin full of sliced beets. (The Parisian Paul was thinking of was the son of an undertaker in Lyon.)

A restless crowd of hotel guests had already gathered at the chain that blocked the dining area. How could these people rouse themselves to eat a banquet after last night's *reveillon?* But the guests already shifted impatiently against the velvet-covered chain, and one stout burgher leaned across the barrier and scooped up an hors d'oeuvre of toast and caviar. His thick-waisted wife playfully admonished him, but finished the last bite of toast from her husband's fingers. A small boy in ski suit and slippers ducked under the chain and snagged a langouste behind a waiter's back. The maitre d' came by and waggled his finger at the crowd, but he was quickly off to the kitchen again, and a woman picked up a stalk of celery spread with cream cheese as soon as he disappeared.

In a little while the crowd had broken through. They elbowed their way to the tables snatching up everything in sight. (Word must have spread through the hotel, for the elevators disgorged fresh commando teams of famished guests, and a party of skiers came running through the lobby from the parking lot.)

The first wave had already scooped up oysters into slings made of napkins and wrestled whole lobsters from their refrigerated nests; the newly arrived had to make do with cold chicken breasts and slabs of goose paté. The oversize Niçoise came apart under the assault, and was soon scattered; the floor slippery with stray cornichons, slices of salami and mayonnaise. The frantic mob crushed deviled eggs under-foot, scattered carrot sticks and celery stalks; olives bounced like marbles to the parquet. At worst it was frightening, depressing at best, but Paul did not turn away.

These are my readers, thought Paul—my livelihood. Tourists rooting in the ice for shellfish, slurping oysters, cracking open lobster claws with their bare hands. Somehow the orchestra started up, perhaps activated by the riot, an accompaniment to chaos—fifteen accordionists, at least, pumping out *Lady of Spain*. Paul was thinking what a swinish place the world was when the telephone rang.

"Oui."

Clearly a woman's voice this time, a better connection. Duff did not come on the line (perhaps out of fear that the phone was bugged), but the voice confirmed an appointment for this afternoon and assured him Monsieur Duff would be delighted to see him. Imagine, thought Paul, having an answering service in Shangri-la.

Now, with the box of cigars in his briefcase (Joan's gift to Duff), Paul stared gloomily upward along the *crémaillère* cable reflecting on their last conversation.

In Joan's opinion Europe, like marriage, was for the birds. "What's a sweetheart like you doing in this no man's land?" (Did she mean: "Let me take you away from all this"?) True, he had escaped the hustling U.S.A. for the same grubby hustle abroad. Paul's theory of exile was that Americans were simply looking for little Americas in foreign places and finding them. But he was different, he wanted to tell her, he had married one of Europe's daughters; he was wedded to the place.

Paul turned from the frozen spectacle beyond the tree line and tried to remember when he might have been like the carefree kid across the aisle. A pair of skis handy, a backpack attached to a lightweight frame; that was the *wanderjahr* way to do Europe: utilize her slopes, play in her sand, sample the wine of the country. But Paul, a travel writer, was no traveler—he was here to stay. He had committed himself to the European dream.

"Short lesson in geology, boys." An American mother three seats away was pointing her ski pole at a V between mountains. "How was that valley formed?"

Paul was annoyed with himself for being critical of every American he heard from a distance. To avoid his countrymen was not enough: he could not bear to see them clicking cameras and scattering travelers checks from one end of the continent to the other. Why did they have to speak louder than they would have at home? Yet they were good people, he was one of them. He tried to think of something good about the woman (she was a *good* mother) despite the superior tone in her speech and the Mickey Mouse ski caps her sons were wearing.

Europe is for the birds. Instead of answering Joan's question, Paul had put the same challenge to her: "What's a nice girl like you ... " The answer was clear-cut enough. "A husband on my hands I'm trying to get rid of." What better reason for renewing her *carte de séjour* than waiting out an alimony settlement.

She loved Duff, she loved him not—in spite of her daisy-petal affection Joan wanted a divorce. Well, Paul knew how easy it was to be ambivalent about Duff. "I always liked Duff," he told Joan—but why had he expressed this sentiment in the past tense? He did not know if he liked Duff or not. He was greatly charmed by the man and vicariously intrigued by what the bastard would pull next. (Pull Paul out of the doldrums, maybe, and into the vortex again.) Duff and his talent for big money. *Is that why I like him?* Duff and his penchant for high places. Follow Duff's lead and you are forever dangling from these slender cables, ostensibly on the way up.

Just then the downside cable car drifted by. As soon as the windows of both cars were adjacent Paul had a composite flash of walking wounded limping home (for there was a ski slope up there, as well as a sanctuary)—two with broken legs, a girl with her arm swathed in a silken sling—but as the car passed, the boy across the aisle did not look up from his soiled paper copy of *The Magic Mountain.*

The boy, in fact, did not look up at all until the car jerked to a swaying halt at the *terminus* platform. Something happened to his mouth, and it seemed as if his tan had faded. Paul followed the direction of the boy's eyes: there was a corpse blanketed in plastic on the platform floor. The passengers shuffled out of the car and stared down at the body, then quickly away—even the American mother was silent. Paul was part of the file of unhappy spectators. Like any of these tourists he considered this a vacation place—he thought he had come to a place of fewer fears.

The corpse was strapped to an aluminum stretcher remarkably like the boy's pack frame, flanked by two somber attendants waiting to escort the deceased to a lower altitude. Paul stared just long enough to measure the cadaver with his eye. It was too long, too thin to be Duff.

Fifteen

This year's Swiss travel poster featured a generous Helvetian sun, but here the ceiling was as low as the leaden sky over Paris, the landscape as desolate as the moon's—no transportation, of course. An ambulance, the only vehicle in sight, was parked tilted in the snow, the driver reading one of those *photo-policiers* with the dialogue in comic-strip balloons. He was unhappy to be disturbed, grunted something short of a snarl and reluctantly pointed out a squarish institutional building with a radar on the roof. It was only a ten-minute walk. A lost mitten hung from a telephone pole added to Paul's distress: he was the lost part of something himself. The chill cut through his Burberry, and the building grew uglier the closer he approached. He had to cross an open field of mud and slush—their version of a moat, thought he.

Paul reached the gate just as the ambulance turned into the drive. It was the same ambulance he saw parked at the *crémaillère* (having just served as a hearse, no doubt), and he silently cursed the driver for not offering him a lift.

The gate to the driveway was open, but the front door was a formidable piece of woodwork reinforced with metal studs. A white-robed nun answered his ring. (Hadn't Joan said something about a nun who carried a pistol?) She wore a ring of keys around her waist instead of a crucifix, and he wondered if the flowing sleeves hid a shoulder holster.

Only after he showed his *carte d'identité* would she admit him into the frigid foyer lined with coathooks shaped like gibbets. Without a word she took the briefcase from him, removed the gift box of cigars and placed it on a dead radiator; she used a pen knife on her key chain to cut through the seal. Paul was embarrassed by the security measures and looked away, pretending interest in a rusted snow shovel propped behind the Bastille door. She clawed diligently through the box: there were cigars inside. When she closed the box and gave it back to him, Paul muttered an ironic *merci*.

They stepped through what appeared to be a bank vault into a steam-heated hallway that smelled of wet fur; then up an ecclesiastical spiral of steps, like the steps that lead to bell towers in Romanesque churches, and into another, narrower hall, through yet another bank vault—the nun unlocking all the way—until Paul decided somewhere along the labyrinth that Duff was a myth that had disappeared with Amazing Growth, and the trip through the maze was a practical joke.

But the tunneling did open out, at last, into the *grande salle*. Paul crossed the vast checkerboard tile floor alone (his guide seemed to have faded into the tapestries) toward the banquet table where two men played Scrabble under an overbright chandelier. The player in the Japanese robe was Duff, with a beard. He pulled off his green eyeshade in greeting.

"Paulie! My favorite wordsmith. How the hell are you?"

When the other player stood up, formally, Duff announced: "This is Mauriac, so-called. We're all anonymous up here. Leave it to the Swiss to hide your name and assets for you."

Mauriac's fierce mustache did not match his wounded expression. He offered Paul a beautifully manicured butcher's hand, bowed out of the game and followed the ghostly nun into the tapestries.

"Belgian," whispered Duff—but Duff was no whisperer, and the word bounced off the walls. "Big munitions man from Antwerp."

Paul glanced down at the Scrabble board where Mauriac had just worked out *coeur* using the "e" of Duff's *remote*—or was it the other way around?

"We play English and French both, but the first time he tried to pull Flemish on me I said to drop dead."

How quickly, bluntly, Duff subdued the competition. Already Paul felt dominated by the Duff persona, overwhelmed by the nonstop monologue, reduced to an adolescent again (though Duff was actually two years younger than Paul), with Duff's familiar paw gripping his elbow, guiding him into an elevator posted STRICTEMENT INTERDIT (strictly forbidden to whom?), haranguing him about the circles under his eyes, his haircut—"You got to get a better barber, you know that?"—leading him down a corridor lined with doors bearing nameplates from *Aragon* to *Zola*.

"Security here is tighter than Fort Knox."

"I noticed."

"At night they switch the electric fence on and turn the Dobermans loose."

Duff pulled a set of keys out of his kimono pocket and unlocked three locks on the door marked *Marot* (next door to *Mauriac*, which explained his Scrabble partner's pseudonym).

"Did you recognize me with whiskers?"

"You look the same," said Paul, "only with a beard."

Flourescent lights flickered on, and they stepped into an eighteenth-century drawing room furnished by a twentieth-century sybarite. The nymphs and satyrs on the wall panels were in character—and the antique French telephone, instead of an intercom, understandable—but the books? Duff's reading seldom went beyond *Barron's*, *Fortune* or the *Wall Street Journal*, but here an entire library of volumes cluttered the desk top, filled a wall of shelves, spilled over into stacks along the floorboards—all in uniform pink jackets, untitled.

Paul noted Duff's world globe, with its one hinged hemisphere (there was a stock ticker inside, no longer ticking of course), and—dead center in the pink clutter of books on the desk top—a miniature guillotine (a paper cutter, apparently, or mechanical letter opener, but actually Duff's droll symbol of decisiveness). Both globe and guillotine were mementos of the great days of Amazing Growth, totem objects Duff had managed to rescue out from under IRS investigators, a militant committee of stockholders and Swiss receivership. Paul threw his Burberry across a Louis XV chair while Duff was on the antique phone calling for champagne.

"Hey, wordsmith," Duff said suddenly. "What the hell happened to you?"

Paul looked where Duff was looking, at the Rorschach stain on his shirt pocket.

"I would've said you were bleeding, except it's blue."

"My pen. The altitude, I guess."

Behind the ragged beard was that down-turned smile Duff reserved for anything cheap. A ballpoint pen offended his sense of style.

"Wait a minute," said Duff, and he shuffled out of the room.

Through the open door Paul saw a bed, unmade, under a damask canopy. Duff fumbled through a baroque armoire of clanging hangers, then returned with a new shirt, still pinned, embossed with the ubiquitous "C" of Pierre Cardin. Duff was a tosser. Paul caught the shirt with one hand, the way a bellboy retrieves a flipped coin.

As Paul changed shirts, Duff remarked, "You're looking thin, you know that?"

Now, thought Paul, he can always say he gave me the shirt off his back.

Duff had given Paul and Sylvie matching butane lighters as a wedding gift. Later he gave them an oriental rug for the apartment in Cannes and a cocktail shaker. Once, for no special occasion, he gave Sylvie an Amelia Earhart aluminum suitcase and Paul the silver hip flask he still carried.

Within a week of the wedding Paul lost his lighter somewhere in the wind-blown sand between Dunkirk and La Panne, lighting a picnic fire of driftwood in the dunes. Madame Chaix owned an apartment at the seaside, across the frontier from Dunkirk, and they spent their honeymoon there at the Belgian coast, of all places—cold, even in August. The two weeks had been perhaps the happiest in Paul's life.

Why the Belgian shore? The air, said Sylvie, was loaded with iodine—it would help protect them against colds during the long rainy fall in Paris. So, after the cold-blooded ceremony in the Eleventh Arrondissement of Paris, they took the train to Dunkirk, and a cab across the frontier to La Panne.

The apartment had a view of the steely Noordzee, but the day they arrived an army of bugs had been transported by the brisk wind and deposited against the seaside window: all they could see was a flying, crawling, incredible mass of shiny red beetles with black lacquer spots on the globular wings.

When the bugs were blown away by a wind from another direction they could look out on the shoreline of candy-striped windbreak canvas with strictly defined rows of beach umbrellas planted in the sand. Sails and flags, kites, bunting and bathing suits. The whole color spread might have been a well-planned tulip field, or an army camp, or

Coney Island. This view of Belgians, Belgians, Belgians (as numerous as the *coccinelles* that had swarmed against the window) was at first comic to Paul, then something of a delight. The holiday crowd was one vast potato shape in baggy bathing costume: no one, it seemed, was under the age of forty or over the age of four. Buttermilk flesh with sunburned noses. Cigars, newspaper and knitting. Their king, Paul remembered, wore rimless glasses and collected postage stamps.

But what a sanctuary it was for newlyweds. They could walk among the masses and be as remote as ghosts. Another secret pleasure Paul enjoyed was knowing this was where Sylvie spent her childhood summers—a glimpse into a part of her life he would never have known.

The canvas city by the sea would be left high and dry at low tide: beyond the speckled pattern of footprints lay a flattened expanse of ocher sand, a green and gray metallic sea. At sundown the leaden sky was a backdrop to an apocalyptic seascape in watercolors. A seminary of youthful priests came solemnly trooping through the sand, and from the west three shadowy horsemen galloped out of the dunes and down the shore.

The apartment was part of an ancient wooden structure squeezed between grim new high-rise apartments. On the walls, bespeckled with sea damp, were sailing prints and maritime charts and ship's brasswork. (Sylvie compulsively kept the brasswork polished.) Plaster dust from the cracks in the walls, and the wind, drifted down onto their dinner table.

When Sylvie went shopping along Nieuwpoortlaan, Paul sat in the Café Albert I trying a new beer every time, a golden tide of beer, not just the local brands—Stella Artois (known affectionately as "Stella") or Ekla or Geuze or Speciale

Aerts, but the heavy brown monastery-brewed Chimay, Orval and Rodenbach—but the imports too—Diekirch from Luxembourg, Tüborg from Denmark, Guinness from Dublin and Spätenbrau from Munich.

La Panne was a place of children. Paul and Sylvie, like children, went to the amusement park called Meli to eat the waffles Sylvie had eaten as a little girl, *gauffres*, with ice cream. The merry-go-round still turned to the airborne piping of a calliope. Paul put a Belgian franc into the slot below a mechanical donkey's hooves, whereupon the clockwork animal brayed piercingly, jerkily lifted its tail and ejected a chocolate bon-bon from its derrière.

The water, Sylvie insisted, was too polluted to swim in, and anyway too cold, so they donned yellow slickers and sailed in the sand yachts called *chars à voile*, skidding along the flat sand at the shore, tilted, splashing through tidepools, powered by wind only.

They rented bicycles and pumped along the tracks behind the streetcar to Oostende, through Nieuport, Koksijde and Krokodiel—little duplicates of La Panne beside the sea, and sometimes a queer-shaped pressurized blower steered ahead of the trolley, blowing sand out of the tracks. That same night they saw the movie *Gejand Door de Wind*, with Clark Gable and Vivien Leigh, at the Minerva Cinema, and Sylvie put a handkerchief to her eyes in the dark when Scarlett O'Hara decided to go back to Tara.

One sad overcast day they hiked into the dunes for a picnic, the only color in sight was the distant rainbow of clouds at Dunkirk, which Sylvie explained was really spumes of pollution pouring out of factory stacks near the sea. They came to the spilled pillboxes and cracked concrete bunkers of World War II, the cement defenseworks broken open by tide and time. Both of them had escaped the war: Paul was too young, Sylvie lived in neutral Switzerland—but now they could safely set up their picnic among the BEWAAR/ DANGER signs and devour with an appetite beyond belief Ardennes ham, boiled eggs, Breughelbroed, Gouda cheese and a single parched herring, entire, a flake of golden sheen on a piece of wax paper, staring up at them with one terrified eye.

Hovering behind a bunker among the windswept dunes they kept close to the fire and listened to Paul's portable radio catch the fading crackle of BBC news from across the channel, mostly news of garden clubs in Gretna Green and how to make homebrew wine out of turnips. Sylvie had brought *French Without Toil* in the picnic basket, and Paul practiced his French for as long as he could endure it. He tried to distract his teacher by dribbling sand over her ankles or tickling her ear with a straw. Sylvie turned suddenly serious, as if the sky had darkened all the more.

"I must confess you this."

"Confess this to you." He was the teacher now.

"Confess this to you. I will never take a lover and you must not, too. I am not what Americans probably think of European wifes—French, above all—that they are light about love, and even permit the *ménage à trois*."

"Not me." Paul was amused. "*Ménage à deux* is all I can afford."

But Sylvie was serious: "You must promise."

He put one hand into the wind and the other on *French Without Toil.*

"Just the two of us, I swear. Until we have children."

He had been thinking about children all week, in this children's corner of the world.

"Only one," she said quickly.

"Only one child? O.K. You sure?"

"I do not want to become just a mother."

"O.K. Only one. But let's work on that one right now."

Paul wanted to make love on the blanket they had spread for a tablecloth, but Sylvie was afraid someone would come.

Sixteen

"Listen, I drink a bottle of champagne a day and my ulcer don't know the difference. There's Scotch, if you want— Black Label, by the way—bourbon, anything—" Duff opened the globe to reveal his liquor stock, instead of the obsolete stock ticker. "But whiskey'll set you up for a nice cirrhosis if you don't watch it, and anyway the ice up here tastes like frozen piss if they forget in the kitchen to put mineral water in the ice-cube trays."

"Nothing for me, thanks." Paul felt his face go warm: he was thinking of the phallic icicle in Joan's hand. "I had a heavy *reveillon*."

"Drink it, it's *curative* for Christsake."

Despite the premonition of heartburn, nausea or worse, Paul accepted a fluted glass filled almost to overflowing with sparkling liquid. The wine had been delivered by that same surly ambulance driver—wearing an intern's white jacket. The silver ice bucket resembled a piece of equipment from a requiem mass. They drank religiously: the champagne was Dom Perignon.

"I brought you some cigars. Your wife sent them."

Why had he said "your wife" instead of "Joan"? Afraid of Duff's ESP, Paul passed the cigar box across the desk, watching for signs—but Duff wasn't showing.

"Yeah, Joannie's all over the place. Where'd you see her?

How the hell is she? You won't believe this, but I still love that bitch." Duff noticed the broken seal on the cigar box and smiled. "Little Sister frisk you? She's a pisser, but she keeps the vultures—like my wife—off me. You realize there's psychos out there that if they can't slip it to me through regular channels would be happy to mail in a gift-wrapped time bomb.

"Let me tell you what happened that time I was hiding out in a hotel in Zurich and this character barged into my suite with a fistful of A.G. stock in one hand and an oyster sheller in the other. An *oyster* sheller. He could've put my eye out! If Hector hadn't showed up in time I'd've lost an eye, I swear."

Hector, another souvenir from the Amazing Growth era, was Duff's bodyguard-valet—an ex-Interpol investigator or former CIA man, or was it the Deuxième Bureau?

"You know what he wanted? He wanted me to buy back his stock! Me, in person—in *cash*. I mean, it was comic in a way, tragic as it was."

Champagne had never depressed Paul before, but now it did. At breakfast he had worked up the prospect of asking Duff for fifty cents on the dollar (he had bought the securities at par); in the cable car he marked the price down to twenty cents, then ten—but now he was obliged to let that particular pipedream fade to nothing.

"Same with everybody, everybody points the finger at *me*. You read what *Newsweek* said? Sure, we played the currency angle, so did everybody else—you have to, to keep up with the gnomes. O.K., we went too heavy into Riviera condominiums and office space in Paris, which took a nose dive just when the dollar did—but the recession was what killed us, and inflation. How can they blame inflation—or recession, for that matter—on *me*? The crunch came and no liquidity, naturally—your liquid assets are too vulnerable to devaluation—and a lot of people got hurt. But try talking liquidity to a guy with an oyster sheller aimed at your eye."

"Did you get hurt?"

"No, I just told you, Hector showed up."

"I mean when A.G. went under."

"Me? I saw it coming. I bailed out." He put a fist into his kimono pocket and pressed it into his groin, where something hurt. "So I was lucky—why crucify me?" He took a medicine bottle from the desk drawer, swallowed a capsule and washed it down with champagne. "You can get this stuff under another brand name in Geneva, and cheaper. Like an ass I was having Maalox and Amphojel imported from the States till I figured out the Swiss're so uptight they got to have ulcers too. It taught me a lesson."

"Live and learn," said Paul, thinking of a lesson of his own.

"You're never too old to learn. I learn something new every day of my life. Take Mauriac, for instance—that's him playing the harp."

"Harpsichord." Paul could hear Bach's "Jesu, Joy of Man's Desiring" through the walls.

"Yeah. I don't know how the hell he got it up here. Anyway, I learned a lesson from him. Never feel guilty. The *guilt* that guy feels. His wife, by the way, committed suicide. Talk about ulcers, he's got *bleeding* ulcers; he one time vomited blood all over the Scrabble board. His stomach must look like a sieve, from the holes he's got in it. All he can eat is baby food and Vichy water. Can you picture Joannie committing suicide if *I* went into armaments?"

Paul could picture Joannie committing something else.

"His daughter ran off with a Dutch hippie. Count your blessings, for Christsake, I told him—it could've been a black. He tells me she called him a killer. Kids today, they don't stop and think. I told him if he didn't sell hand grenades to cannibals, somebody else would—but he's too full of guilt to listen."

Duff tilted backward in his padded swivel chair to pull at a cord behind him; as the drapes parted, the room seemed to open into white. The sudden light hurt Paul's eyes: the snow could have been powdered soap. He thought of his dream, the bedtime story he had worked up for Christine: a king trapped in a tower of ice. It was a fairy tale not to tell Duff: Duff was the king of this tower, under an evil spell of his own conjuring. Paul examined the panorama of jagged mountain peaks—a circular set of them, like teeth—and wondered, am I inside the tower looking out, or outside looking in? He shuddered, from cold or fear. Simply to say something to Duff, he said, "Nice view."

"I quit looking at it." Duff jerked sharply at the cord: the drapes shot back in place, the room closed in again. "Staring at all that snow, I was beginning to feel like a footprint." Then his face brightened, as if he were inspired: "How the hell's Sylvie?"

"Fine," said Paul, relieved that Duff knew nothing of the break; it was the last thing he wanted to discuss with Duff. The grapevine did not extend to this altitude.

"And the kid?"

"Fine, great."

"Beautiful, beautiful." Restless, still swiveling, Duff suddenly scooped two cigars out of the gift box and flicked one toward the sofa where Paul sat. Paul was annoyed with himself for catching it; he was already smoking a cigarette.

"I never smoke cigars."

"It's curative, for Christsake." Duff sliced off the end of his cigar in the miniature guillotine. "Cancer? Don't believe everything you read. I read in *Time*, by the way, where the CIA hired the Mafia to try and plant poison cigars on Castro —can you feature that? Never trust anybody."

Paul put the cigar in his Pierre Cardin pocket: "Maybe later."

"Except Joannie. I'd trust her on cigars, but not in a divorce court. We got married in Nice—I ever tell you?— so I got her over a barrel. We're covered by the French Code Civil, it dates back to the Middle Ages."

Paul nodded grimly.

"I mean, those guys knew what the score was. She can't touch me for franc one, and she knows it—but she still might try to pull something."

"She says she still loves you, and you say—"

"She say that? When'd she say that?"

"Yesterday. And today you tell me you love her. Why divorce?"

"We can't stand each other, that's why. I love the bitch but who can live with her? She lines up seventeen chicks she swears I screwed to try and screw me with them. It's *her* that wants the divorce. Ten thousand A.G. stockholders left holding the bag, on my back, now *she* wants to get her hooks in me too. Instead of trying to patch things up she comes up here with affadavits, trying to serve *papers* on me—as if I didn't have enough fucking subpoenas from the SEC, IRS, class actions and Senate investigating committees—what kind of wifely devotion you call that?" Duff shot up from the chair and stalked the room, nudging stacks of books aside with his slippered foot. "What gets her, what gets *everybody*, nobody can lay a hand on me up here. I'm signed in. Not even the Swiss can touch me. The fence is electrified, they got killer dogs on patrol all night. As long as I don't step a foot outside, I'm a free man."

Paul leaned his head against the scrollwork of the sofa and sneezed; his feet were wet.

"You allergic? There's a Czech allergy specialist up here." He poured more champagne, a medicinal dose. "There's even shock treatment, if you need it. Anything. You get a sudden urge to pray or something, they got their own private chapel that's an exact miniature of the Sistine Chapel in Rome, downstairs. A high colonic and massage guy comes in every day—or a masseuse, if you want to mix sex in, only for her you got to make an appointment—but I don't like anybody putting their hands on me, it rubs me the wrong way, though I hear it calms your nerves down. So far I'm coasting along nice enough on Equanils and sauna baths.

"You ask me if I'm a sick man." (Paul did not remember asking.) "Aside from a little gastritis on my stomach if I eat too much seafood, and a very very mild duodenal, I'm better off healthwise than when I was twenty. So why'd I sign myself in here? Listen, I could direct fifteen holding companies from up here, all on that one phone, and not risk the coronaries guys in New York and London are dropping dead from. Also, I admit, I'm trying to lower my profile so I can show my face again in the investment community. Up here nobody bugs you.

"Take yourself, for a minute—and I mean this as a heartfelt word of advice from a long-standing personal friend of yours, but you got the look, Paulie, of a person under pressure. My advice to you—" but when he saw the shift in Paul's expression, he switched to his favorite maxim "—only never take anybody's advice—not even mine.

"Let me tell you something." And he told, for the twentieth time, how he made a fortune in hula hoops, operating out of a phone booth in Philadelphia, no cash up front. Duff had total recall for names, details, sums invested and account

numbers of clients—every business deal he ever made was
engraved on his memory—but, like Grimwald, he could
never remember telling a story twice. "... then I had it
straight from Disney in person the next big fad has got to be
Davy Crockett. I take the man's advice and end up stuck
with four warehouses full of coonskin caps. Lucky I had a
head on my shoulders—" Duff was playing with the guillotine "—and didn't panic. Never panic. My worst moments,
I never panic. I cut my losses and collected the insurance." As Duff splintered toothpicks and decapitated safety
matches, Paul remembered Joan telling him Duff had set fire
to those warehouses himself. "Cut your losses, man, is my
advice to you."

Paul's losses were not the same as Duff's—and, anyway,
never take anybody's advice. Duff tossed a book at him and
Paul regretfully caught it.

"The sky's the limit with this thing." With one of the
last intact matches Duff lighted his cigar, then puffed it into
life. "Publishing."

Paul did the only thing he could think to do with the
book: he opened it.

"Just read the first paragraph, give you an idea. I don't
mean *write* the things, fabulous wordsmith that you are—
I can get hacks in Hamburg, Ibiza, Canterbury for Christsake, to do the dirty work—I mean publicity, your old slot,
back in the saddle again—only anonymous this time."

"I don't think—"

"What's the matter? You're thinking money, I can see it
on your face. O.K., here it is: no piddling salary to start—
nothing on the books that way, keep the IRS in the dark—
just free-lance me a few ads at first, help me on the fucking
editorial end, and as soon as the ball starts rolling I cut
you in on twenty percent of the net, no less."

"Duff, I—"

"—got a job, I know. Writing travelogues, I heard, for peanuts. But this is back in the majors where, believe me, before the year's out you'll be making four times what you made before and ten times what you're making now.

"Listen, I remember that boat ad you did for A.G. with bales of money piled on deck. The good ship Go-Go, you called it, with a fat cat captain bellowing through a megaphone—what was it?"

Duff waited for Paul to reveal what the captain had bellowed, until finally Paul winced and said, "Come aboard."

"That's exactly what I'm saying, for Christsake, come aboard!"

Duff seemed to have forgotten the good ship Go-Go went down with all hands—except the fat cat captain. To get out of the firing line of Duff's relentless gaze and hard-sell salestalk, Paul turned to the book in his hand. The pink jacket covered a paperbound volume called *Lip Service*, by J. DesLevres. Paul sneezed.

"You got to take care of yourself, Paulie. That weight loss worries me, I mean it. Stay here a week, a month, as long as you want, on me. Call Sylvie, tell her it's business, she'll understand. In fact, I made reservations already. I got you booked into the Camus, the guy that had it had a heart attack.

Could that have been Camus under the blanket on the platform at the *crémaillère?* People were dying of heart attacks just to make room for the Phantom Inspector.

"Want to hear something funny?" (No, thought Paul.) "There's a masochist in the Sade suite. No kidding. You should see the doll he has in, weekends—black boots and a tool kit full of whips—Little Sister goes over her with a geiger counter."

Paul's gaze had wandered from the book. He had changed into René de Cygne, interviewing the man who first thought up package tours to the moon.

"Just glance at the first page, give you an idea what we got going."

Impossible to fantasize in the same room with Duff. He did not want to let the dismay show in his face, and to keep from watching Duff play obscenely with the cigar he tried to read the cheap print—but his mind was elsewhere. Already in transit, he was planning how he might get the couchette window open on the train back to Monte Carlo, to get a breath of air.

"You know something? A wide mouth on a girl is a sure sign of the hots. Gunda's got this wide mouth. She comes up weekends on the same train from Berne with Puss-in-Boots. Would you believe me if I told you that little item you're reading was written by a female?"

He remembered the boy in the cable car reading *The Magic Mountain*. I've never read Thomas Mann, thought Paul. I've never read Proust.

"Notice how Joannie's got a very small mouth."

And lovely hands, but wide astonished eyes. What do wide eyes on a girl mean?

"You really ought to get a load of Gunda, but she only comes up weekends. Call Sylvie." Duff pushed the antique French telephone across the desk. "Tell her you got tied up. Gunda's German. She's the one that wrote the book— would you believe it?"

Nothing Duff could say, nothing he could offer, would bring Paul one millimeter closer to Sylvie—he lingered and listened out of a lopsided notion of courtesy and respect.

"No more French broads for me, or Italians. Remember

that Italian chick I promised to put in the flicks that tried
to haul me into court? On a *rape* charge, for the love of God.
Never trust a broad. Joannie's the only girl I ever trusted,
bedwise anyway." Duff opened a desk drawer to use as an
ashtray. "You want a girl? You look like you need one. I'll
send Azziza over, once you get checked in. Camus was Algerian, you know that?"

I've never read Camus, thought Paul.

"Our whole marriage she never once cheated on me, not
once." Duff took a sphygmomanometer out of the open desk
drawer and began rolling up one sleeve of his kimono. "I
don't know what it was—love or loyalty or if she was just
too uptight to—but I had Hector check on her and she was
faithful as hell from the wedding on. We got married in Nice
—did I tell you that?" Duff wound the strap around his upper arm while Paul abandoned the ill-printed text of *Lip
Service* to watch. Duff squeezed the rubber bulb suggestively
(the way he did anything with his hands: caressed a champagne cork before nudging it loose, cracked his knuckles in a
Laocoon sprawl of fingers that looked like arms and legs),
saying, "But now I don't know. Lately she's all over the
place. I'm thinking about putting a tail on Hector to make
sure *he's* not shacked up with her."

Paul, who had managed to erase Joan from his thoughts,
pictured her now putting a Swiss franc into a slot, in bed
with Hector.

"Jesus." Duff was staring sourly at the gauge. "Every time
I think about Joannie my blood pressure shoots up. I'm
thinking about bugging both their rooms, but what I should
do I should stop thinking about her."

People ought to just meet and ball each other . . . Paul had
looked away while Joan draped her auburn wig over a water

pitcher—did she do that when she was with Hector? No truth or ethics to it—like *Lip Service*—and damned little desire.

"I still can't picture my Joannie making it with an ex-cop."

Paul could. And he felt an odd flash of jealousy, a twist in an unexpected place—perhaps because he had, in the end, put Sylvie in Joan's place. Forget that. But Paul remembered the bullet-faced bodyguard with particular loathing. Hector had the damndest hands—hands like Mauriac's, as a matter of fact. The classic predator with a scoreboard he kept in public, Hector used to boast out of the side of his mouth about the eager thighs that had opened to him. Well, Paul's tepid conquest was nothing to boast about. The ceremony itself had been as mechanical as the bed's electric vibrations, a children's game—but if the game was an attempt to get back at Duff, or get to him, it was not exactly child's play. The performance, he reflected, was worth just about what Joan had invested in the vibrations: two Swiss francs.

"And if I start putting a tail on Hector I could end up having to put a tail on the tail." Duff had just reached for the cigar when it went off in his mouth.

The concussion knocked Duff's head back, his eyeshade askew. His face was streaked with charcoal above the new beard. Meanwhile the harpsichord in the next room tinkled to a halt, but Paul's ears were still ringing from the shock.

After a moment's surprised silence Duff staggered upright.

"The bitch," he groaned. "She could have killed me."

He lurched from the room spitting out burned shreds of tobacco, the rubber tubing from the sphygmomanometer still dangling from one arm.

Paul sat stunned by the explosion. It took him several seconds to rouse himself and follow Duff into the bedroom:

he found the victim seated on the edge of his bed, crying into a towel. Duff's slippers had fallen off, his kimono had come undone; a baby spot at the top of the canopy illuminated the bald place at the back of his head.

"Get me an Equanil, will you Paulie?"

Paul's final service to Duff would be to find the bottle of pills in the drawer of his desk, and pour the man a champagne chaser. Then Paul took a towel from the bathroom, dipped it in the cracked ice from the champagne bucket and placed the wet towel across Duff's forehead. Duff lay back on the bed, in blackface, the damp towel like a turban that had come undone, the kimono open to a vulnerable strip of mottled flesh. How fragile he looked lying there on the bed with his hands folded delicately at his crotch. Paul applied the capsule directly to Duff's tongue and lifted his head so that he might swallow the champagne without choking.

Duff, his face a burned smear, looked up from under the towel and said: "Paulie, I'm afraid to die up here."

Paul was obliged to avoid Duff's eyes.

Marivaux. Mallarmé. Loti. What demons plagued the occupants behind those doors? No one stepped into the hall to ask about that curious blast (perhaps the rooms were soundproof—but no, he had plainly heard Mauriac's harpsichord). There was no one to stop him from taking the elevator marked STRICTEMENT INTERDIT. As he walked beside the painted panels of the downstairs hall he expected Little Sister to appear from behind a Chinese screen, to materialize in a vapor out of the umbrella stand—or was she secretly watching through a nymph's frightened eye in one of the *trompe l'œil* panels? But he passed from vault to vault unchallenged, an invisible man, opening the bolts himself from the inside.

He stepped into the chill outdoors and sneezed. He did the stations of the cross in reverse and was about to wade through a stretch of new snow beyond the gate when he encountered the sullen ambulance driver—in denim butcher's apron now, and earmuffs—wheeling a garbage can along the drive. They exchanged a look, then Paul found the cigar in his shirt pocket, tossed it to him and was pleasantly rewarded to see the man catch it and smile. There was a Zen koan here, the answer to which promised instant enlightenment, a riddle he hoped to solve in the cable car on the way down.

Seventeen

He had resigned himself to exile, knowing in his soul the term of separation was only temporary. Solitude had become a familiar state: he saw himself in mirrors, or recognized his knees or feet in the bath—but otherwise he filled the empty space unaware. His small apartment was comfortable enough —and comforting in a way. If only he could sleep nights.

He sometimes forgot what day of the week it was, but knew the month was January, and he survived an unbroken series of perfect January days—calm sea, cloudless skies—by a careful, ritual respect for routine. As if preparing for a seige —but with the belief it would end happily—Paul began to lay in supplies.

He bought himself a soldier's sewing kit and sewed the burst heels and toes of his socks into tight little knots. He learned to use the temperamental washing machines at a laundromat in Menton and even bought a can of Vool-eet, which turned out to be Woolite, at a *droguerie* in the village, so that he might wash his sweaters in a bucket of cold water.

He set up his bachelor's ménage with a kind of fussy interest that took his mind off the larger issues. Shopping at the outdoor market in Menton was a colorful distraction; even wheeling a supermarket cart along the cluttered aisles of Casino or LeClerc was a sufficiently rewarding chore. He lined his garbage can with pages from the *International Herald-Tribune*.

At first the Mazarin sisters were hurt that he should give up their demi-pension meals, and bitter at having to reduce his rent by one third, but Paul gave as an excuse the many professional meals he was obliged to eat elsewhere, and the fact that he could not always get back to Roquebrune in time for the evening meal with them. Also, he had little appetite at night, after sampling the heavy restaurant offerings of stewed rabbit or poulet roti, a gigot or bouillabaisse, with the inevitable selection of cheeses and dessert. Now Paul made his own scrappy little suppers from paté and cheese and fruit he kept in the screened-box *garde-manger*; or he boiled up a pot of rice, or occasionally made a tomato sauce, and prepared omelets with mushrooms or ham. Eventually the elderly sisters—too senile and forgetful to nurse a grudge —dropped their wounded expression and began offering him Provençal recipes, and lemons. Besides, they had another border at the table now, a bachelor.

Mr. "Fish"—as Paul thought of him (his name was Collins, but the sisters pronounced it *Colin*, a French fish) rented the *grenier* room above Paul's apartment. A remittance man from Maryland, he had been living in Europe since World War I—where he lived during World War II, Paul did not know. To avoid taking meals with the new pensionnaire was another one of Paul's reasons for withdrawing from the dining arrangement—not because the gentleman was offensive in any way (though Paul instinctively went out of his way to avoid Americans in France), but his dress was depressing: he wore the somber black garb of an unsuccessful undertaker. His French was perfect, elegant even, but he spoke in a voice from the grave. There was something macabre about the man, and Paul feared he carried death's calling card in his pocket.

The Mazarin sisters, however, were delighted with their Monsieur Colin and flirted with him in their sly spinsterish French way over tea and wine and supper. They called him *"notre écrivain,"* for it was said he wrote. Paul had formerly been *"notre journaliste,"* and received their exclusive attention at table, so he wondered if he could be jealous of the harmless old man. It was a thought he might have analysed at another time (the unexamined life, Paul agreed, was not worth living), but lately he was too confused in his stricken soul to accept the fact of a new flaw in his character.

Meanwhile, to boost fortune and morale, he tapped away at travel articles. He delivered this month's Phantom Inspector report two full days before deadline. (Grimwald was eating an ice-cream cone when Paul delivered the manuscript, and was so startled he spilled droplets of mocha-vanilla on his neck-tie.) With time on his hands Paul toyed with the backlog of miscellaneous trivia in his repertoire, and did a short article on smuggling at the Menton-Ventimiglia border station, for a French trade journal called *Turisme*. He did his own translation out of Mansion's *French and English Dictionary* and the *Petit Larousse*, without Sylvie's help, and thus emboldened went on to work up a five-thousand-word script under the name René de Cygne for a Club de Voyageurs brochure. (Advertising required making a few words go a long way, but a journalist learned to write reams about nothing—in either case, Paul discovered, you lied.) He did not allow himself breath between productions to debate the moral considerations here, for he was becoming (or had been, all along) an inspired liar. The piece he wrote for the club was a completely invented puff about the Hôtel des Voyageurs in Leysin, and he took a perverse pride in having described a hotel where he had never been a guest. The gala holiday meal he documented was the one he witnessed from a telephone booth in the lobby—the riot deleted, the vulgarity suppressed—and when the check came from the club's *Loisir & Plaisir* (enough to pay Miss Bishop back, and buy a portable radio), he decided it was the best thing he had ever written. You should write fiction, he told himself. I do, he replied.

Under the freakishly potent January sun he could sit shirtless on the balcony, a straw hat to shade his eyes, espadrilles on his feet—like a peasant, like the Mazarins—typing, listening to his new radio or just watching the shadows of clouds float across the flat sea, between drinks. He missed his tape and record collections of Bach and Handel and Vivaldi, but often he could tune in a bit of baroque on France-Musique, or even get an entire Bach cantata, when the garrulous radio commentators let up talking self-consciously about music and put a record on. When nothing else offered he tuned to a local pop music station (he found total silence too ominous to bear) that spun out twelve hours of numbing soft rock interrupted from time to time by a girl with a sexy whisper who broadcast news flashes of catastrophe or offered Mini-Mir at *mini-prix* (but gives the maximum) in the same seductive tone, as if she were dressed in negligee.

He had become superstitious, and was careful not to smash the spider that lived in his typewriter, certain the little beastie brought good luck. He was almost convinced, too, that the Mazarin sisters might be right when they insisted an electrical appliance still used current, mysteriously, as long as the plug was in—so he unplugged the radio when he was not listening to it.

For a time he discussed with himself (aloud, one of the regressive traits that came from living alone) whether or not to buy a used car—a little *deux chevaux* perhaps (put together with paper clips and baling wire, though serviceable) —but he feared he would end up with a piece of junk, knowing how aggressively the French drove their cars—and, anyway, it would be something of an admission of defeat for a man who continually told himself (aloud) he would have his family and automobile back any day now.

Sylvie made no gesture toward a reconciliation, but she did not give any overt sign of hostility, either. They still communicated, by telephone and mail—though it was invariably Paul who called, and their conversations were full of awkward pauses and empty spaces between *bonjour* and goodbye. He could see J-P any Wednesday he chose, for as long as he liked—but on neutral ground. Sylvie had just sent a photostat of J-P's latest report card, along with his drawing of an astronaut, U.S.A. written across the space helmet and *"Pour Papa"* written at the bottom of the page. She forwarded Paul's mail (the most recent: two postcards from his brother, a sailor on a Mediterranean cruise—one card from Tunis, the other from Greece—who promised [or threatened] to visit them when he got to France), but no communication from his wife hinted at a truce. However, Paul preferred stalemate to warfare and kept his eye on the heavens, looking for a halcyon bird.

Nevertheless, he did not sleep nights, and he was inclined —like Sylvie, in the early days—to hypochondria. If he did doze off he might suddenly awaken with a fearful sense of suffocation, or a peculiar numbness in his feet, or migraine— but all of these nocturnal symptoms disappeared by daybreak.

Often he spent the long insomniac hours listening with the dedication of a scientist to his own irregular heartbeat.

Lately he lingered over news articles in *Le Monde* or the French edition of *Reader's Digest* concerned with cancer, cholesterol and kidney machines. The current school of medical journalists was unanimously agreed that coffee, cigarettes and alcohol were the leading causes of heart attack, and Paul made heroic attempts to cut down on all three. He still prepared an ebony tinted hair-raising espresso filter in the morning, but drank only that one cup and for the rest of the morning—especially while he worked—resorted to tea. (Until he read in *Figaro* that tea contained as much caffeine as coffee or more, and he slipped back into the habit of sipping coffee at the typewriter.) Trying to limit himself to one pack of cigarettes a day he tried chewing gum, but it hurt his teeth, and if he bought fewer cigarettes he was obliged to borrow from Mr. Fish before the day was out. He did adopt the inspiring motto Never Drink Before Sundown, and followed it scrupulously (except for wine at lunch, "in the line of duty"), but when he checked the levels in his collection of bottles under the sink, or threw out the empties, he found no hard evidence of reduced intake. He seemed to be starting later, but drinking more.

He bought aspirin, for the first time in his life, against migraine; he bought a bathroom scale and a thermometer.

To keep from hallucinating he bought a reproduction of a painting by Paul Klee and hung it on the wall opposite the bed, so that he might see it first thing in the morning, last thing at night. The work haunted him in a completely satisfying way—he could see it with his closed eyes. Though he would never solve its geometrically abstract puzzle, it crowded out lesser visions and gave his agitated mind a focus. Paul Klee was Swiss, and the painting a mixture of cold colors and fire (the grays flecked with silver, like Sylvie's eyes, in a certain light); Paul thought he might find his wife in it, eventually, but caught only occasional glimpses of himself.

Late afternoon was still his favorite time of day: no demons pursued him then, and he could imagine his vexations sinking with the sun behind the cypresses and stucco villas of La Turbie. Unfortunately some entrepreneur had perched a tourist hotel on the cliffside of the Tête de Chien, a sterile eyesore of steel and glass (awarded two stars by Grimwald, in an early issue of the *Guide*) that looked as if it might slide down into Monte Carlo any minute. What disturbed Paul was that the setting sun was trapped in its sheer glass sides for thirty minutes at a stretch, and during this unnerving interval he stepped up his drinking, impatient for the earth's rotation to resume, waiting for that last blaze of blood red to pass beyond the hotels of this world and sink peacefully into another hemisphere.

For days the vision of Christine eluded him, perhaps because Fish sat late in the garden now, but one empty afternoon a cloud of fluttering butterflies filled the garden, a snow flurry of small white *papillons* blown over from Corsica on a North African wind, and Christine was suddenly poised in the midst of them. Her features were as indistinct as ever, and she would not return Paul's ardent stare, but what rendered substance to the vision was that a butterfly landed on the little girl's head and remained there until she disappeared.

Eighteen

Sylvie did at least meet him halfway, and they met in the Jardin Albert I, just off the Promenade des Anglais in Nice. J-P was perched on a wooden pony making the slow-motion circle of the carousel, sucking on a *baton de rélgisse*—a pharmaceutical substitute for candy and the last thing in the world Paul knew of that cost only fifty centimes. Sylvie sat in her suede coat on a park bench nearby, her hands in her pockets (the weather, after this morning's burst of winter sunshine, had turned sullen). She looked out of place in the empty park, but as self-contained as ever. They exchanged a semiformal *bonjour* but did not kiss. Just as well, thought Paul, for he had taken a cognac in Menton to fortify himself for the rendezvous.

J-P waited until his horse glided to a full stop before he dismounted and ran to greet Papa. (Paul noted only one other customer for the carousel in this weather: a small girl riding the horse behind J-P's, but she was not Christine.)

"If it should rain," said Sylvie, "be sure to pull up his *capuchon*."

Paul was scheduled to take J-P to the zoo in Monte Carlo. Sylvie drove them to the bus station behind the Casino Municipal; she would meet them there at 5:30. Did J-P have his sugar? *Oui.* Paul should not forget to give J-P his *gouter*—forty grams of bread—at four o'clock. At the station she handed over the packet of bread to Paul and a sack of peanuts to J-P.

"Remember, the peanuts are for the animals only."

J-P was forbidden peanuts by his doctor: he put the peanuts in the pocket of his anorak, and Paul put the bread in his own pocket, then slapped the bulge, to reassure Sylvie he had it, and there was no hole.

Paul stood aside while J-P kissed his mother *au revoir*, then Sylvié drove off.

Actually, Paul had no intention of taking J-P to the zoo in Monte Carlo. When they got on the bus marked "Hippodrome," J-P—a compulsive reader—asked, "Is this the correct autocar, Papa?"

"You like horses, don't you?"

"Yes. Above all with cowboys attached to them."

"No cowboys this time, no Indians either. But you'll like these horses."

"What horses?"

"At the racetrack. The horses run very fast and people bet money on who wins."

"Maman didn't give me any money."

"Never mind. I've got money for both of us."

"*D'accord*," said J-P, and during the short bus ride to the hippodrome he sucked contentedly on his *reglisse* while Paul tried to make sense of a French racing form.

Not that he would need to know the form, the record or past performances: he had decided to try the System passed on to him by Mr. Fish. Fish himself never attended the races at Cagnes-sur-Mer—"I cannot abide crowds," he said— but sat in the garden in a protected spot next to the rabbit hutches he called his "sun trap" and pored over the racing pages of *Nice-Matin*. Paul suspected Fish eked out his slender existence by pension check and an occasional money order from family in Baltimore, but he was too short of ready cash to risk betting on horses. He made "mind bets" at a safe distance from the track, no risk involved. He kept careful notations of every bet he made, then compared the results in next day's paper. (Paul had seen his notebook of mind bets, and was impressed.) Every racing season he won a small hypothetical fortune this way. "I have a system," he declared, and he was willing to reveal the secret to Paul, after Paul had graciously invited him to use his shower one day. Fish had no bathing facilities in his tiny room; Paul had the only shower in the mas—and when Fish emerged from the steamed-up bathroom, damp and glowing (and smelling a little less obviously of the grave), he offered, gratis, to describe the system to his neighbor, no strings attached.

Fish's voice was a unique instrument: a *basso profundo* as hollow as an echo from an empty tomb: "You, my dear fellow, have the advantage of following the parimutuel board at the track. I, alas, must deduce the approximate odds from the often incomplete newspaper listings of the morning line. Thus your opportunity to maintain a consistent series of second-favorites, *sur place*, will be much greater than my own haphazard guesswork."

(When he was not making mind bets on horse races, Fish claimed to be writing a definitive history of Flemish art. His room was directly above Paul's apartment, yet he had never heard Fish at the typewriter—perhaps the author wrote with a quill pen.)

"At the last possible moment before post time, place a five-franc bet on the second favorite 'to win.' If this horse happens to come in first, pocket your small winnings—*bien sur*, the net profit is bound to be small at this stage—and start over again. Same bet, five francs, on the second-favorite in the following race."

"Right," said Paul. According to Fish, his book would prove once and for all that the masterworks attributed to Rubens were actually painted by the obscure Frans Snyders.

"If the horse loses, you merely double the bet to ten francs in the next race, twenty francs on the following, and so on—

in other words, keep doubling up on each subsequent race until your second-favorite comes in again. Amazingly simple procedure, but highly successful. All based on the inexorable law of averages."

"I see," said Paul. He had not so much listened to what Fish was saying as how he said it—the sepulchral voice with a slight remaining trace of southern accent.

"Statistically—my own statistics, I never trust any others— you will have at least three second-favorite winners in any one racing day. The longer you lose, the better off you are— you actually *win* by losing, since you have doubled, quadrupled, et cetera, your bet until you *do* have a winner. The beauty of it is your winnings have also doubled, quadrupled, et cetera."

"I see," said Paul, who did not. He could never fully understand the modern business principle of winning by losing: *Grimwald's Guide* losing money to create a tax shelter for his other profitable enterprises; Duff going bankrupt to become rich.

"In the long run—" Fish was saying, and that phrase seemed to be the key to it all. In the long run. Patience was the watchword. We will all be winners in the sweet by and by.

With only 240 francs in his billfold, Paul decided he had next to nothing to lose. The track was only open three afternoons a week, and it occurred to Paul this minimum investment in time and money might bring in a welcome supplement to his mediocre earnings as the Phantom Inspector. If he understood Fish correctly (but he did not), he calculated that a mere seventy-five francs would carry him winnerless through four races at least. This was an experiment only (he kept telling himself)—a warm dip, not a cold plunge. If he did not have a winner by the fifth race he would write off the seventy-five francs—just as he had once written off fourteen dollars he lost at River Downs, in Cincinnati, the one and only time he ever went to a race track—and abandon the whole idea.

A stream of racing fans poured from the parking lots and train station next to the hippodrome, but the bus driver cut through the crowd like a cattle drover, lavish with his horn and brakes. His shaken passengers were deposited at the admission gate: PESAGE 10 FRANCS, PAVILLON 4 FRANCS. Paul took a pavilion ticket, J-P was admitted free.

"Is it like *le cirque?*" asked J-P.

"More serious than that," said Paul, who thought it might turn out to be a circus after all.

He tucked J-P close in, one hand on the nape of the boy's neck, afraid to lose him in the mob pushing toward the hall beneath the grandstand. Despite the bus driver's daredevil performance, they had missed the first race. The betting hall was a grim cement structure completely unadorned except for the ubiquitous French warning signs that spelled out what the patrons were obliged to do and what was *interdit.* An unfriendly scene, Paul decided, despite the mass of hopeful humanity milling through.

He tried to unravel something called the *code theorique* that flashed from a flickering parimutuel television screen. He could not distinguish a blurred 6 from a blurred 8, and had to ask J-P's opinion—whose guess was as good as his. The favorite must be number 3, with odds (Paul supposed) at 2 to 1, but which horse was the second-favorite? Suddenly the odds flickered off and an ad for thermo-massage came on. To make matters more confusing, he had forgotten to buy a program outside (there were none for sale inside the gate) —however, he was perhaps better off not to know anything about the horses, not even their mostly American names. The System, Fish had stressed, dealt with numbers only—not horses or jockeys or past performance. But when the *code theorique* flashed on again Paul still did not know what the numbers meant.

Finally, with the help of a toothless paralytic in a wheel chair; Paul found out number 11 was bound to be second-favorite, at odds of 4.50 to 1. He hustled J-P away from the obliging paralytic (the child was beginning to stare) and joined a long line of bettors snaking forward to the window marked PARI 5 FR. (Fish had said to wait until the last possible minute, but how was he to know what the last possible minute would be?) Because of the inevitable reverse funnel of French line jumpers, the slow shuffle forward seemed to last forever, until at last Paul placed a five-franc coin on the anonymous number 11 to win.

For luck Paul gave J-P the ticket to hold and, for dear life, J-P held on to it. The grandstand area was as crowded as the betting hall: patrons seated on cushions of newspaper (for the seats were slab concrete) or pressed together—in superstitious solidarity, for human warmth?—along the rail. A few meager furs hung on the ladies with the brightest lipstick, one man in a hundred wore a pair of binoculars dangling from his neck; there was a sprinkling of pimps and touts and a contingent of Arabs with at least two gold teeth apiece. Like tourists, racing fans must belong to some underground international brotherhood; Paul was reminded of River Downs some fifteen years before: the same mixture of casual money in casual clothes rubbing against the shabby patchwork of the down-and-outers. It was a crowd gone to seed.

He was surprised to see so many children. The kids, of course, were oblivious to the racing fever all around them. Small boys scavenged for tickets discarded by losers of the race before; girls were skipping rope and playing *cache-cache* in the crowd. There were even babies in carriages, mostly asleep, but the newborn nearest Paul lay solemnly awake staring into the scudding clouds while his distracted mother jotted calculations in the margin of her racing form.

Paul and J-P stood on the lowest tier of the concrete grandstand with a distorted view of the flat oval and a stretch of Mediterranean hanging mirrorlike, a mirage above, yet beyond, the track. The horses—according to the loudspeaker—were off.

"I don't see," said J-P, and Paul hoisted him to his shoulders.

There in the middle distance, just this side of the wind-blown sea, a moving mass of something broke along Paul's line of vision. He listened to the word from the loudspeaker, but—since he did not know the names of the horses—the hysterical jargon of shifting positions meant nothing to him. It was not until the homogenized mass of horseflesh rounded the near turn that Paul could distinguish the shapes of small men clinging to the beasts—then, in the stretch, the clump elongated into a series of horses with no less than a dozen legs each and a blur of numbers, none of which was 11. By the time his eye had registered a pattern of color other than one churning mass of mud brown, the scene was blank again: the race was over.

"Did we win?" asked J-P.

The numbers 7, 3 and 14 lighted up the board in the infield.

"Not this time," said Paul. According to Fish it was better this way.

With number 9, Paul did win in the third race, and they were rewarded with a frustrating wait in the long line that led to the *caisse*. He collected a modest twenty-two francs ("The net profit is bound to be small at this stage," Fish had warned him), but by then Paul needed a cognac, and cognac was selling for ten francs. There was a bar beyond the topmost tier of seats: a small sad booth with two shelves of exotic bottles, one table with a sign above it: *interdit* to sit at the table without buying a drink. Nobody was sitting at the table. The eager barman was already leaning forward, but before Paul could order he realized J-P would want a Coca Cola, also *interdit*—he couldn't drink without offering his son a drink, and he couldn't offer his son a drink. He backed away and the disappointed barman went slack again.

It was a relief to have a loser in the fourth (standing in line was the worst of it, win or lose—no wonder Fish never came to the track). Anyway, you win by losing. But J-P was beginning to flag: Paul saw him glance enviously at the kids scooping tickets from the ground.

"Just one more race," Paul promised him (and himself), "and then we go."

From the rear of the betting queue Paul was feeling sorry for the harassed cashier bent over her electronic ticket punch —to be middle-aged, and tired, and tied to a relentless device of the workaday world—for even from this distance he could see the gray growing out of the center crease in her golden hair, and as he drew near he noticed she was obliged to keep an electric coil going to warm her feet. But when he was about to place his bet, it was her turn to feel sorry for him: his billfold was not in his inside jacket pocket. He tried another pocket—queasily, without hope—then every pocket, every crease.

J-P's face turned pale, his eyes misted: *"Tu l'as perdu?"* He reverted to French in times of stress.

"Let's look," said Paul, as cheerfully as he could manage, and they stepped out of line.

Walking back, bent, searching under the feet of those still in line, they found nothing but discarded tickets and wadded Kleenex.

"Maybe the other line. Where we bought the ticket for the race before."

But the cashier working the five-franc window shook his head: "*Pas ici.*"

One of the twin gendarmes patrolling the hall took Paul's name and address, then led him to a white-haired harridan who guarded the public washrooms (TOILETTES 0,60)—she looked closely at Paul, as if his game might be to use one of her booths without paying the sixty centimes. She unlocked a door marked OBJETS PERDUS at the rear of the lavatory, no more than a closet with shelves devoted to a mongrel assortment of lost-and-found canes, compacts and *carnets*. There was a mason jar of ballpoint pens, a broken umbrella, a collection of combs, a Bible bound in green, one glove and four billfolds, empty all.

"*Merci,*" said Paul, after one brief hopeless sweep of the display. As they left, the matron scowled at them—she had expected a tip.

But he had no money, no papers either. It was a good thing (if anything was a good thing anymore) the gendarme had not asked for Paul's *carte d'identité* when he took down his name and address. They did that, the French—a stolen *carte* was no excuse. His press pass from *Grimwald's Guide* was lost as well, but that could be replaced. Even J-P's *gouter* was missing—the forty grams of bread—lost or stolen along with the billfold. It was after five, and J-P should have had his ration an hour ago.

Nightmares follow an inevitable progression (there is no

relief), and by grim logic J-P should be suffering a malaise by now: he was pale, his nose was running—Paul expected him to faint. No money to buy a sandwich, no sandwiches, in fact, for sale. In desperation Paul took the chewed-up butt of *réglisse* out of the boy's mouth and began feeding him the forbidden peanuts, one peanut at a time, as if by strict rationing the nuts could do no harm.

The paralytic rolled by in his wheelchair, and Paul thought of asking the man for a loan, but asked the time instead, and offered him some peanuts. He realized Sylvie was already waiting for them at the bus station in Nice. But I don't have bus fare, he tried to tell her, by telepathy.

J-P read the anguish in his father's face, and was crying— like his mother, tears without sound. Paul stooped to wipe his eyes and fed him more peanuts. Should he have sugar? They would have to take a cab, if he could find one, and ask Sylvie to pay. Maybe he would go up to the stone-faced gendarme again, to borrow cab fare, but this time he would surely be asked for his *carte d'identité*.

Am I completely unhinged? He was casting about; his head turned sharply from one hopeless direction to the other: to the ground, in case the billfold was lying there; to the sky, for another kind of miracle (or the hope he might be swallowed by the threatening El Greco crack between the clouds), until a desperate glance at the paddock section brought a vaguely familiar figure into focus.

Chantal (he did not know her last name), from the Tahiti Café.

He called to her, he waved. But Chantal was watching the fifth race; Paul could not even hear the sound of his own voice over the loudspeaker, over the crowd. A chain fence separated the pavilion from the paddock area, but Paul remembered a passageway between the sections. Alas, there was a guard, a six-franc surcharge to pass through. *"Pas d'argent,"* Paul explained, exposing his pocket linings. Could the little boy go through to deliver a message to a friend? The guard shrugged. *"En principe, non,"* but the guard deliberately turned his back as J-P dodged past.

Paul went back to the chain fence to watch: J-P quickly found the lady in lavender, politely touched her elbow and pointed to Papa on the other side of the barrier. She smiled; she recognized him, she waved.

Lovely the way they walk. She had taken J-P's hand: legs, hips and shoulders doing all the right things. In France even the prostitutes have style.

"Quel Malheur," was her response to Paul's misfortune; her eyes reflected genuine dismay. (And he had not even told her the half of it.)

Paul could not help thinking how unfamiliar the gesture must be to her (considering her metier) as she pushed a folded fifty-franc note through the chain link into his hand. Though he was not even sure what her metier was. She had some mysterious understanding with the bartender at the Tahiti, a Corsican dwarf. Paul had never really seen her with a man in all the months he patronized the place (it was just around the corner from *Grimwald's Guide*). Perhaps the Tahiti Café was a convenient drinking spa for her as well as for him. (No, that wasn't the story—but never mind.)

She was leaving the hippodrome anyway—*"J'en ai assez"* —it would be no trouble to drop Monsieur Paul and *le petit* in Nice, on the way. There were no taxis, there was no choice. The car was a tiny red Fiat Sport the same shade as Chantal's lipstick.

She drove with French *élan*, gesturing extravagantly as she talked (she talked about horses, and men), one hand on the wheel—Paul feared the bracelets on her wrist might catch in the dashboard knobs. They were only forty minutes late—but would Sylvie think of it as "only"?

Sylvie. It was not until they drove up behind the Opel in the municipal parking lot that Paul wished he might be sitting next to someone else, that the Fiat might be some less obvious color.

He escorted J-P to the family car. Chantal, with a breezy gesture of farewell, bracelets jangling, drove on—but Paul was watching Sylvie's face, her winter look. The expression was a familiar one: the lips thin, the nostrils narrow—but he could not remember her eyes as gray as this, though it may have been the reflection of the gray Opel, gray pavement, gray sky after all that lavender and red.

J-P was already in the car. He would have a tale to tell Maman—too late to suppress that: Paul was a negligent liar in his own backyard—but he did want to get a word in with his wife, his version of the afternoon. He had not realized the motor was running; he was obliged to take a quick step backwards as the car started and edged him to one side. Sylvie circled him, as if to avoid hitting a careless pedestrian in her path, but with a speed so deliberate he knew she would run him down without a thought if he attempted to violate her right of way.

With the fading backflash of J-P's face pressed against the rear window (the boy did not realize he was being carried off: he proudly displayed a stack of losing tickets at the window, a salute to Papa) Paul was left standing in the vacuum between two speeding vehicles driving in opposite directions. He should have asked Chantal to drive them to the border at Menton where he could have fled with his son into Italy. No, he was a hapless victim of circumstance—miserable but not desperate. He could not commit a kidnapping in the name of melancholy. But the wild thought brought on its own punishment from above. The sky cracked open with a snap and, before he could seek shelter in the bus station, buffeted him with a barrage of hailstones.

Nineteen

"I'm not getting any younger," said Grimwald—an uncharacteristic admission, his sleeves rolled down for a change. (Just saying it, seemed to have aged him ten years). Paul racked his brain for an upbeat reply, but all he could manage was: "None of us are."

Yet the old man was dressing younger: he wore a bright plaid jacket, and horn-rimmed glasses instead of rimless. Miss Bishop had told Paul that Grimwald drove a Porsche now, with a horn that played the open notes of the Marseillaise.

"One of these days, Paul—" but before Grimwald could get into the future, he told an inspirational tale from the past. It was the story of how he first went into business for himself (selling embalming fluid, of all things), a story that Paul had already heard before. He could never understand how a man with Grimwald's computer memory could forget how many times he told the same story. "Never as happy in my life as when I signed up that first funeral director, and made my first fourteen-dollar profit, free and clear."

Paul assumed he still had the fourteen dollars.

Then, with a leathery smile and his arms open in a gesture of largesse, he told Paul the film festival was all his this year.

"She's all yours, Paul," he said, offering him the Cannes Festival and all its works. (Every May, at festival time, Grimwald took his Rudolph Valentino tuxedo out of polyethylene and went off to the movies with the naïve delight of a five-year-old headed for Disneyland. The film festival had always been Grimwald's baby.) He took off his horn rims and rubbed at his eyes with huge thumb and forefinger. "Sight's not what it used to be, you know. Forty films in two weeks is more than these old peepers can take any more."

The smile turned to a pained grimace when he mentioned increasing Paul's word rate, beginning next month.

"Few more francs, nothing extravagant. Not my nature to toss money around, for the sake of tossing. I'm no Santa Claus—you know me—but I'm no Scrooge either. Now, you're a family man . . ." and here he paused significantly, waiting for Paul to confirm what he already suspected—but Paul was not confirming, so Grimwald went on: ". . . and a family man this day and age the cost of living what it is (and going up daily, darn it) could use, I know, a little extra cash."

"I appreciate—" Paul began, uneasy in the presence of so wrenching a generosity.

"Nothing," said Grimwald, and he flung a hand into the air-conditioned air. "Nothing at all." When the lapels of his plaid jacket flew apart, Paul noted the sporty rainbow-striped suspenders. "Think nothing of it."

Paul was ready to forget the whole thing, when Grimwald's hand came down from the heights, the fingers thrust forward like a karate blow: "A deal then?"

What deal? The festival, Paul supposed—the word rate increase. Grimwald's contracts were verbal, but his handshake was the same as a signature in blood. Paul braced his arm for the bone-crushing ceremony, but this time the handshake—as sincere as ever—was not hearty enough to hurt.

Grimwald rose from his manuscript-laden desk and towered over Paul a moment, cast his considerable shadow over Paul, wavering—like a tree, Paul thought, about to be felled

—then strode purposely to the window that looked out on the Grimaldi castle. His manner was distant, vague.

"One of these days, Paul . . ."

Had he slipped into the past again, or was he a man (in his own words) "ahead of the season"?

"Someday, my boy, all this will be yours."

Did the old man mean *Grimwald's Guide,* or the kingdom of Monaco?

When Paul passed through the outer office Miss Bishop scrambled out from behind her desk. It was the first time he had ever seen her legs: she wore some kind of ersatz wartime stockings. She waved an envelope at him. Inside was his press pass, to replace the one he'd lost at the racetrack, as well as the April check (at the old rate) for the Phantom Inspector and some film festival brochures.

"I'll see you to the elevator," she said, in a breathy whisper, a conspiracy.

Must have heard the news through the intercom, thought Paul. Wants to wish me well, in my new eminence.

They waited in the hall together. Miss Bishop looked so unfinished without her earphones, so awkward in those stockings.

"He's not well, you know."

"No, I didn't." He immediately recalled the diminished handshake, the faltering stance.

"He's on the phone daily, with his doctor. It's frightful of me to listen in. But I do." Miss Bishop's blue eyes brightened with tears.

"That bad?"

The elevator came, but Paul did not get in.

"Oh, that dreadful word doctors use."

The elevator closed and traveled elsewhere. Miss Bishop

had come out without her handkerchief, so Paul gave her his. She was too well-bred to repeat the word. Paul was unaccountably sad; he suddenly loved the garrulous old man, or maybe had loved him all along.

Then, as if she were ashamed of this Mediterranean side to her British character, Miss Bishop abruptly stiffened and handed Paul his handkerchief back. He would like to have comforted her, but she was having none of that now. He realized she would not long survive her employer; she would, in turn, die with her boots on, alone.

He went down in the next elevator with Miss Bishop's tears in his pocket.

Twenty

Once upon a time Paul and Sylvie had been as happy in this town as they had ever been. (And as miserable, he reminded himself.) Cannes. After the long train ride from Paris they stumbled into the Beau Séjour—a lucky place then, with Fernandel for a desk clerk—where the halls smelled of lime, the big bare room was beautiful, the bed a bed of flowers. (Next day Duff whisked them off to the Majestic, but never mind.) It was called the Hôtel du Commerce now, and the management had a fixation on *fleur-de-lys*. In another year, when the wallpaper peeled and the plumbing failed altogether, the porter would stop polishing the brass rods on the stair carpets and the owner would decide whether to try for another face lift or simply allow the old ruin to find its true level—or level it. Knowing you can't go home again, why had he decided to stay here?

Since he had no intention of attending the Palais des Festivals at night, when *tenue de soirée* was required (he had no evening clothes, and he could see the same films at the morning and afternoon showings), he might have commuted daily from Roquebrune, only an hour from Cannes. Except for the steps. There were at least a thousand stone steps from the Mas Mazarin to the little train station at Cap Martin— he would do the festival, he could not do the steps. All the best hotels in Cannes were booked, overflowing with the festival crowd, even if Grimwald would have allowed for an expense account, first class. (Anyway, Paul was not prepared to rub elbows with the show-biz set.) So he chose the Hôtel du Commerce, on an impulse. And, although Cannes was— as the crow flies—halfway from Roquebrune to Ys, he had in some inexplicable way doubled the distance between himself and his wife. Cannes was just another kind of exile.

The SNCF tracks ran right through his room. He had a view of the uninspiring Rue de 24 Aout—what could have happened in France on the twenty-fourth of August to name a street about? (It might have been when Paul and Sylvie stayed here.) Between trains and traffic jam *klaxons* on Jean Jaures, water pipes flushed down through the building, shutters crashed shut. At night a mortar barrage of motorcycles backfired, cab doors slammed and Germans argued with waiters in the café below his window. Hotels across from train stations are not recommended for insomniacs—make a note of that, for *Grimwald's Guide*.

Grimwald: he mourned the man prematurely. Duff, Grimwald. Paul took these things personally. If the stalwarts of the world were going under, what about weaker vessels like himself? He lived in a state of suspended animation, if not downright dread.

Alone in his gruesome room Paul assumed the corpse pose (Sylvie's specialty, known to relax your tensed-up Hindu); he lay under a single sheet, toes up, rigid as a frozen asparagus, as if practicing for the mortuary. Do you close your eyes or leave them open? He closed his—otherwise, by the flickering neon of the photo shop across the street, he kept seeing the damp Rorschach on the ceiling where somebody's bidet leaked—did it drip still? would he drown? The pose had never yet eased him to sleep, but it did distract him from smoking for an hour at a time. Something incorrect about the breathing, no doubt. It was an exercise that called for breathing through one nostril at a time—but sea level was treacherous to Paul's sinuses: he felt lucky to be able to breathe at all. Inevitably the corpse pose turned Paul's thoughts to Grimwald; he had to give it up. Anyway, sleep was not the most precious state to wish for: awake, vertical, eyes wide, you could always try for numb. A hotel was no place to play dead; it was where you telephoned from and changed razor blades. He would sleep at the movies.

A platoon of photographers beseiged *Documentation* ahead of Paul, but he was in no hurry. They mostly sported chestnut-colored mustaches with sideburns that came within a centimeter of the mustache tips. Photographers dress remarkably alike, thought Paul—workaday denims was the uniform of the day, today. There were pockets, he noticed, sewn into their denim shirt sleeves, and they all wore soft suede desert boots and mostly motorcycle-cop sunglasses. While they asked for printed invitations to tonight's Gala and automobile stickers that said Film Festival (so they could park in no-parking zones) and had to know what time Otto Preminger's plane arrived in Nice, Paul wondered what they carried in the sleeve pockets.

The hotess at *Documentation* reminded Paul of the fairy godmother in J-P's copy of *Pinocchio*: she was of a certain age, her hair tinted blue (*la fée aux cheveux bleus*). She dealt with the photographers as if they were a rowdy kinder-garten class—bright children, but manic—and eventually swept them and their leather mailbags of camera gear into the corridor, into elevators, bound for the Palais terrace to take photographs of the members of the jury. That left Paul, and a condemned couple: a South American journalist and his wife sent by a government that had just been overthrown, representing a newspaper that had been closed by the putsch.

Madame Documentation looked wistfully at the South Americans, sighed, and took Paul next. She had his folder open in an instant, but her eyebrows were creased when she said: "But you already received your accreditation."

"Was it sent to the *Guide?*"

"No, it was given to you personally. Look, you signed for your mailbox key."

Indeed, there was his name: *Paul Swanson.*

"But that's not my signature."

"It is not your name?"

"It's my name, but I didn't sign it."

She smiled faintly and took a vitamin C tablet from a bottle in her desk drawer, for strength. She checked his passport—yes, the name was Swanson; true, the signatures did not match.

"Maybe there's another Paul Swanson at the festival," suggested Paul.

"The Paul Swanson who has been accredited is with a publication called *Grimwald's Guide.*"

"*I'm* with *Grimwald's Guide. I'm* the Paul Swanson the *Guide* sent to cover the film festival."

"There is no other Swanson at your publication?"

"No. Swanson is me. I'm Paul Swanson from *Grimwald's Guide.*"

"*Bon,*" she said, but her smile was gone.

"Why don't you call the *Guide?* They'll tell you who I am."

"*Bon.*"

While he waited for the call to go through Paul stared out the open window past the cloth-of-gold (or was it chain mail?) drapes to an incredibly ugly apartment building, newly built, where the Miniature Golfcourse used to be. Five years ago he and Sylvie wheeled J-P in a *pousette* from hole to hole, playing a Sunday game of miniature golf—but the garish stucco structure spoiled his vision of that Sunday.

Madame Documentation was talking to Miss Bishop on the phone; then Paul talked to her.

"Is that you, Paul?"

"I think so. But I'm beginning to wonder. Seems like there's two of me."

He turned the receiver back to Documentation and it was affirmed: yes, that was the real Paul Swanson who had spoken.

The South American couple listened to all this with pained sympathy and complete comprehension. It had happened to them. Nobody was who he was, nor what he represented.

The good fairy with the blue hair had accepted Miss Bishop's word that this haggard journalist wearing one black sock and one brown was, truly, the one and only Paul Swanson of *Grimwald's Guide. On a dû faire erreur.* Madame D would hustle up duplicate accreditation for the genuine Phantom Inspector. Perhaps the original press pass —which had somehow gone astray—would show up soon, lost and found, and be invalidated. Another journalist, in a rush (journalists are always in a rush), had possibly picked up Mr. Swanson's credentials by mistake. Paul would have to come back after lunch. He did not want to come back after lunch (he was in no hurry, but he knew the South

American couple would still be there, and the thought depressed him), but he did not say this to Documentation. He had learned in France never to disagree with Documentation, never upset a bureaucrat before lunch, never quibble. A *oui* could turn to a *non* at the drop of a *pourquoi*. But he could not resist asking the fairy with the blue hair, "What did he look like?"

"Who?"

"The man who signed my name."

"I don't really recall. There are so many of you."

He thanked the good lady and managed to get out of the office without looking at the South Americans. Later, dabbling at a *salade Niçoise* at a café in front of the *gare maritime* he realized he had crossed the path of another ghost— an evil spirit this time. His double had followed him here. The other Paul Swanson carried the I.D. Paul lost at the racetrack, and now a false Phantom Inspector haunted the streets of Cannes.

No strain, you hallucinated as easily but in a different way at the movies. The films, maybe, from the day before blended into a montage of today's Greek partisans crawling for their lives over barren hillsides to disappear into a cloud of dust and machine-gun fire and emerge L.A. cops from yesterday's drug bust or a team of Swiss astronauts in moon suits scrambling over the same turf. Egypt's vapid vamp from last night's spectacular was spectacularly like the frumpy London model from the 9:00 A.M. showing or Tokyo Rose at noon. These movie beauties were variations on a paradigm, pretty faces telescoped in one, and when they stripped—as they all did— their interchangeable bodies were this year's Miss Universe, as glacially perfect and remotely impersonal. (He could never find Sylvie up there—beautiful in too private a way.)

The Wolf Is Not Native to the South of France

Put a Greek sheepskin on yesterday's armor-plated hero and you had the same man in today's travesty, their deaths identical (they all died in this season's scenarios); he had not watched a believable death yet because he knew the current corpse of a double agent turned counter counterspy was tomorrow's resurrected Renaissance prince. (All the while an old man was dying for real in unbelievable Monte Carlo.)

With a movie projector looking over his shoulder, Paul's visions no longer came out of thin air.

The Grande Salle of the Palais des Festivals was the great bedroom of Cannes (and the Salle Cocteau a great little place for a snooze), where he could drift with the flicker in the quiet velvet-roped press section with its oversoft beauty-rest contour seats nodding yes to whatever banal presentation today's nation presented; yes, yes for as long as he could keep his eyes open, then float—if the wrong image went on too long—to cool Iceland with his eyes closed remembering the film before this one to keep from being burned alive in Brazil. Ah, and the big bad noisy film with a restless shifting unhappy audience. Drift off even with the remote cackle of foreign dialogue and inevitable background gunfire lulled into the most perfect damned near dreamless sleep of all. Not even the carnations planted in the newly sodded orchestra pit wilted till the end, and he survived along with the plants in artificial darkness and air-conditioned air: nobody dies at the movies. It was a daily trip back to the womb, it was a daily Trip: cushioned in foam rubber in darkened auditoriums he slept the unnatural sleep of the drugged, sheltered from stark daylight and the shock of outdoors for as long as he wanted to hide—reel after reel after reel—the way an outcast sleeps off a drunk in the back rows of a double-feature Bijou.

By the second week there was a stewpot of pornography to swim through, but a professional moviegoer, even a novice, shrinks from no vice, though it be the ultimate boredom—yet Paul found himself inspecting the skin flicks with more than a voyeur's interest, with some vague stirrings between the legs, a little live reaction to larger than life action in technicolor cartoon ballooning above his head. His hardons reminded him of the sexual desert he lived in, a wasteland below the waist.

He thought of priests, he thought of Grimwald. Hadn't he read a treatise among the journalistic literature of cancer scare about the self-destruct of sexlessness? Something about sperm backup that set the cells out of balance and slow death by denial. No wonder priests wanted to marry now.

Back at the hotel after a heartbreaking tale of teenage gangbang on the banks of the Ganges (or the Amazon, or the Mississippi) he heard the Whistler in rehearsal—a mysterious whistler was lodged at the Hôtel du Commerce—warming up on an orchestral arrangement of the theme from *Forbidden Games*. Paul felt his toes scrape unpleasantly against the muslin sheets, a relief to know he could at least feel—he would have to trim the nails but lacked the will to bend himself at the knees. He touched his genitals, the source of exquisite pleasure in the past, to reassure himself his equipment was still there, and still flesh, for his face had turned to plaster, almost agreeably so. His brain was cluttered with jarring images from the giant screen of rape along the river bank, and he tried to put together remembered bits of what the rapists down by the riverside had accomplished accompanied by the eardrumming of hard rock and the snide asides from seats on either side of him, but all he got was jump shots of unrelated relationships and the Whistler's piercing background music to the home movie of his own. No way to work up a satisfying arousal in this narrow bed to prevent sperm backup, the priest's disease, Grimwald's fate. Nothing doing here. The hardon from today's matinee did not take at night.

The condition I'm in, thought Paul. Even Onan must have had sufficient muscle tone, a steady pulse and the need to spill his own seed. For Paul there was no release in sight. His penis shriveled in his grip, drew back from his fingers, withered and was transformed into a mushroom while the Whistler switched to a sad slow version of the theme from *Gone with the Wind.* He could not even masturbate without the image of his wife to rouse him, but he had neither strength nor will to dream her up out of the dark. When he turned the bedlamp on and examined his thin pale full-length form, he discovered one of his pubic hairs had turned white.

The press room offered no sanctuary, no corner to hide in; but it was an escape from Hotel Paranoia, a place to type with the reassuring clatter of the Telex in the background instead of the Whistler's impromptu concerts. Somehow Paul contrived to spin out movietone news for Grimwald on one of the Olivettis (with an AZERT keyboard) screwed down to a writing table. He was childishly surprised to watch the pages spew out of the machine with common-sense sentences arranged in double-spaced order that did add up, more or less, to a movie review. It was beyond him how he could manipulate the alphabet into these consistent word games; but he did, daily—his only triumph. He scanned the *Herald-Tribune, Nice-Matin,* the *London Observer* and *Le Monde* searching for conclusions other than his own, but their reviewers only confirmed his slack observations; they were in the same bag. Did these correspondents, too, doze off in the dark and work up a film review from the first reel only, the details filled in from xeroxed handouts stuffed into a press box? Paul's style (and theirs) was a coalescence of the current hot-air school of graffiti art—*X directs Y with a heavy hand; however, for the lighting alone . . .*—pretentious, far-fetched, even comic. I have low enough standards, thought he (tapping away at the tripe) to have made a lot of money in this world.

Within minutes his mood swings could jolt from passive depressive to hyperactive paranoia. He would seek the crowd along the Croisette with the herd instinct of a lonely tourist; follow the Dior lovelies lounging on the arms of bronzed escorts in black tie down the Great White Way of pure light between the Carlton Hotel and the Palais des Festivals where policemen in riot helmets held back the fans, and Paul. He was content to mingle, his press pass safely out of sight, until he might catch the eye of a single cop, their glance held one breathtaking moment (*"Je vous connais,"* said the policeman's eye) and Paul fled to the nervous solitude of an empty café. At a press conference for a director who had transferred Dostoevsky and Dickens to the screen (and was about to crucify Balzac next) he spotted a face in the crowd that could only be Hector's—had Sylvie hired a private detective, and why? In the men's room Paul met a pop artist into film making now, he said, and available for interviews, but Paul zipped up in panic and escaped without washing his hands.

The false Phantom Inspector could have been anyone, and Paul thought of seeking the fraud out, shaking his hand. On Rue d'Antibes he searched the anonymous crush of pedestrians for that one someone who might be tailing him, but the tail inevitably turned out to be a hustling prostitute or an Italian selling sunglasses.

He avoided people he knew: Luis from *La Prensa* and the lady (whose name escaped him) from *Christian Science Monitor*. Seated at Les Noailles, where he often took lunch, if anyone he vaguely recognized approached, he hid behind the Bible-thick special festival edition of *Variety* pretending to translate the show-biz code without moving his lips. Once, under the market sheds off Rue Louis Blanc (where Sylvie used to shop when they lived on Petit-Juas) he thought he saw his old conçierge carrying a net bag full of *poireaux* (a woman he had always admired, *une brave femme* with an idiot son to bring up), but he ducked out between the fish stalls to avoid talking to her. And he avoided, too, Dr. Gaillard getting into his Maserati on Rue des Etas-Unis— Sylvie's neurologist—the last person in the world he wanted to talk to. (Yet he checked the driver of every brown Mercedes that passed, looking for Grimwald, until he remembered Grimwald drove a Porsche now.)

He wore his plaster mask in public. He insinuated himself into the microcosm of the Carlton lobby to pick up stray pieces of additional dialogue to play back in his mind when the big screen went blank and the houselights came up.

"Three-hundred fifty thou split three ways is what?" "A piece of shit." "So what?" "He don't know from nothing, so don't let the threads dissuade you." "So?" "Knows Nichols, knows Dorpierre." "So I said look."

"Look, I said, what kind of person do you take me for?"

Paul lingered near the slow-motion revolving door that sliced and bracketed the crowd into solitaries, then put them back together again under the banner 50 GOLDEN YEARS OF TECHNICOLOR.

"Like," said the woman with sequins on her eyelids, "if I was after her husband—"

"So?"

"Have you seen her *husband?*"

The word HUSBAND hung in the lobby up there with 50 GOLDEN YEARS. Paul sat with his back to the Mediterranean checking his faulty watch with the lobby clock as if there were some place to go, watching the pimps and producers and prima donnas file out of the elevators.

"GG goes for it, and that's two thirds of the initial outlay."

"Would've got layed but he was too pissed to."

"A dog. You read the treatment?"

"*Tous les cons du monde ici.*"

"From Denmark, with an artificial snatch."

"Listen, I got you a seat just two rows back of Ursula Andress. Think of me when you sit comfortable."

The first time he saw the Canadian (with the face of a grave robber) was in the Carlton Bar, early, before the eleven-o'clock apéritif crowd came down, so quiet you could hear one ice cube click against another and the hum of the air-conditioner warming up.

"I got a film showing in the Salle Cocteau tomorrow," he told the bartender. He was a producer from Toronto—Tarranta, like a French horn fanfare. There was a miniature white poodle tied to the leg of his bar stool.

The bartender nodded. Everybody had a film showing tomorrow. *Tamarra.* This week everybody in Cannes was a producer.

"The girl I got in the film does it seventeen different ways."

"I did not know," the bartender submitted, "there are so many ways to do it."

Later, in the Carlton Grill, the Canadian had a table facing Paul's. (Paul ate there for old time's sake: he and Sylvie used to have lunch at the Carlton Grill; the same food as the dining room but none of the formality and half the price.)

"The girl I got in the film—" the Canadian was telling the waiter, but the waiter had business in the kitchen, so the Canadian began talking into a tape recorder "—sitting here in the south of France, André Malraux across from me."

He looked like a lumberjack John Wayne, and Paul began seeing him everywhere, with his poodle, with everybody. Their eyes never met, but Paul knew the Canadian knew he was watching him. If the Canadian carried a false press pass in his pocket, he gave no sign.

The Russian film was about a poet and a hydroelectric dam, in Vladivostok; and at the cocktail party for the press a sweating director presided over a buffet table on the terrace of the Palais where the stunned guests melted like waxworks under the midday sun. The Canadian was there, in a see-through net shirt, feeding paté sandwiches to his poodle.

"Had a sell half the timber in Alberta to finance the fucking thing," he was telling the Russian actor who played the poet.

Paul eased away from the buffet scene with his paper cup of vodka and melted ice down the Palais backstairs until he came to an empty Radio Monte-Carlo sound studio where cold silence was a blessing.

The Canadian came to the Yugoslav slivovitz party with a teenage gypsy from the Spanish film. Paul saw him that same night, in a polished shantung silk suit, at a sidewalk table in front of Gaston & Gastonette with an Italian starlet with hair in her eyes; he was telling her the plot of his next production: the hippie wedding of an Air Canada stewardess and a Penobscot Indian. Next day he was waltzing down the gangplank of a yacht at the Quai St. Pierre with the poodle (wearing a green turtleneck sweater) under one arm and a bottle of champagne under the other. He had his picture in *Nice-Matin* scuba diving from the Carlton pier.

Paul went to the Clôture Gala at the Casino with the idiot hope of deadening a two-day headache with gin and tonic and celebrate the show's closing, but somehow spilled his first drink in the jostling crowd and did not bother to go back for another. The light flashing off the silver platters of hors d'oeuvres hurt his eyes, he thought he heard the Whistler through his headache.

Outside, wandering the Croisette, he discovered he was still holding his empty gin glass—and when he was about to ditch it behind a royal palm he heard the familiar moose call and saw the big Canadian moving up, the poodle on a leash, his lumberjack arm wrapped around Joan Duff.

Joan did not see him: she was staring up into her tall escort's nostrils, giggling about something the Canadian said. Paul skipped ahead, out of sight behind a boat in drydock. Joan Duff. ("Yeah, Joannie's all over the place.") He felt a burn on his neck and dodged out from under the acetylene sparks of a paint-removal torch. Then he found himself standing in line, like an amnesiac, for the last boat to Ile St. Honorat, a short *aller-retour* across the bay.

Twenty-one

An island at day's end—even without a drink, ideal. Cannes was completely obliterated by the intervening Ile Ste. Marguerite—where the man in the iron mask had languished—

a solitary yacht bobbed at anchor between the two islands. Paul moved against the flow, along a wide path bordered by eucalyptus: rows of cultivated lavender on one side, a vineyard on the other. After each cluster of tourists was flushed out of a separate bower by the darkening sky (and sent plodding back to the boat dock with portable coolers and folding chairs) an eerie silence came down out of the trees. Rusted paint-can lids twisted in the wind to keep the birds out of the monastery garden. An Eden was what Paul had come to Europe for, like the monks.

But he came upon a mutilated agave with dates and initials carved into its leathery leaves, and ahead of him two teenage girls strolled holding hands, emblems sewn to the hip pockets of their jeans: hearts and dollar signs. Enough of that. He turned off the path in another direction, toward the shore, where a medieval tower faced the pirates from Corsica, but no defense on the northern flank. At the shore a man in a cap with a plastic visor urinated out to sea between two fixed whiplike fishing poles. Children were dropping balloons of water from the topmost window slit of the tower; no one walked below.

The paths converged and there again were the two girls with their quaint embroidered buttocks. Paul turned down the arcade along one cloister wall where tourists on the stone benches were addressing picture post cards with the concentration of philosophers. The monastery trading post smelled of lavender after-shave. One of the girls, her heart on her hip, was pulling the bell rope at the cloister door. In a moment a slit opened and the face of a Santa Claus peered out.

"*Je regrette, mes enfants—*" but visitors of the female sex were not permitted behind the cloister walls.

As the girls turned indignantly away, Paul went to the

gate, intrigued. The monk's breath was sour, his eyes as bloodshot as Paul's—yes, the gentleman might make a brief visit of no more than twenty minutes. The last boat to Cannes left at six. When the door swung open Paul was surprised to see the monk wore a faded khaki uniform, a cap and bicycle clips. He thought Cistercians wore white. A Santa Claus prays for us, thought Paul, dressed as a Western Union messenger.

Once there had been a thriving order of Cistercians here, but now there were only thirteen monks left. (Paul had a flash of monks playing badminton under the eucalyptus trees after the tourist boat left.) The last of something.

"We live in perpetual silence," said the chatty guide (who had perhaps received dispensation), "We pray five hours daily." They tended their vines and cultivated lavender. When the white-bearded messenger left to answer another summons, Paul wandered across the enclosed garden of broken stone relics—Greek, Roman, Phoenician—found when the monastery had been restored, to the chapel, lighted by a single taper. He stepped inside, knelt at the far corner of a rear pew, not so much to assume an attitude of prayer as to make himself inconspicuous. On a raised platform were two rows of narrow wooden stalls where the monks sat during mass. A stark bare cross, the silver gleam of a microphone on the altar. Only thirteen left. Paul tried to convince himself—in the silence, in the dark—that the last shall be first.

He wondered if they would have seen last night's fireworks from Cannes, celebrating the Brazilian carnival film.

Well, they had found a way out of the world—just this side of suicide. Better than that, if you believed. Paul suffered from a lack of belief. In anything. And there was no way out of the world: look at Duff. Paul looked at Duff in the dark, and then he saw Grimwald.

A tall thin figure rose, and stepped out of his stall. The monk's cowl was down, and Paul was startled at the resemblance. The moment of peace passed. Pray? Father forgive me, but I don't know how.

Anyway, it was time for the last boat back. And his headache was gone. Outside the chapel a stone gargoyle stuck out its devil's tongue at him.

Twenty-two

All the little tricks of routine were restorative: taking the typewriter out of its felt-lined case, setting the margin indentations, rolling in the first blank sheet. But this time his lucky spider rolled out of the carriage, smashed flat against the page. Damn. He pulled the sheet with its stain of destruction out of the machine, crushed it and threw it across the terrace. The only thing against an omen was a drink. But whatever he drank lately burned the roof of his mouth and left an acid aftertaste. And when he drank he began seeing comets out of the side of his eye like the UFO's in the Klee painting. There was half a bottle of pastis under the sink, and despite its side effects the stuff could be depended upon to do its numbing work. He put the typewriter back into its coffin.

Paul did not have the steady hand he once had, pouring a drink. He splashed a dash of water into the glass, and left a ring.

Paul and Sylvie had met over a spilled drink on a ship called the *Bonnes Nouvelles*, out of Marseilles, on a Mediterranean cruise. It was the concern Sylvie showed over the wine stain on his pants that first made her so attractive to him. She had been so serious, so anxious. She sprinkled table salt on the wet place, assuring him this always worked with wine stains on tablecloths, and asked if his pants were tergal or cotton. So humorless, so intense—the initial evidence of her Swiss practicality. Even later, in the depths of a crippling depression, she kept her check stubs straight, her social security receipts in chronological order. There was something inexpressively endearing about her sense of how the things of the world are done. How could he have resisted placing his scatterbrained life in her competent hands?

He blinked, to clear away the blue asterisks before his eyes—then Christine appeared in the midst of them, and he smiled, amused that he could see the little girl and Fish— in his sun trap—could not.

Did anyone travel on ships any more? (The 747, as Grimwald pointed out so often, had changed the face of the universe.) There was a post card on the table beside his drink (Sylvie faithfully forwarded the mail) showing a fleet of ships idling in waters of Neopolitan blue and his brother's childish scrawl: *Long time no see. When we get to France I'll look you up. Fuck Europe, Neal.*

From Sylvie there was a note so brief as to be almost insulting: *Call me about Wednesday with Jean-Paul.*

They had met on the *Bonnes Nouvelles* and she sprinkled salt on his wine stain, now she sprinkled salt on wounds.

Sylvie came from one of those mixed cantons of Switzerland that combined a French outlook with Germanic thoroughness. She took life with a seriousness almost comic in its exaggeration. When the ship stopped at Genoa, and they had dinner ashore, she said to him: "If I should die in a foreign place I do not want my body shipped back to Switzerland. The expense is unbelievable." Paul had learned by then not to smile. She did not laugh easily, and if he laughed at something she did not find funny she was hurt, and would brood, thinking he mocked her. Humor was not as international as Paul once supposed.

Within a month they were in Paris, living together in Paul's small flat, planning to be married. She did not want to go to America, but she would go there if he insisted. A wife follows her husband. (But not to Roquebrune.) Her first lover, the only one (she insisted) before Paul—and he believed her, he believed her still—was a Rumanian-French professor of Ancient History. (The affair, she implied, was ancient history too.) He was offered a post at the University of Texas lecturing on Babylonian dreams. But she had broken off with him. (Did she regret it now? Dreams sell well in America.) The professor had taken his dreams to the U.S.A. and Paul had brought his to France.

It took six weeks of heartnumbing paperwork to arrange for a civil ceremony at the *mairie* of the Eleventh Arrondissement: Sylvie kept the accumulating documents in a pink folder, and they rejoiced over each new acquisition like collectors of exotica. Paul could not remember the year of his father's birth and made a guess of it (why should a mayor of Paris be concerned with that?); he once misspelled his mother's maiden name and a sharp clerk spotted the inconsistency, to set the process back a week. If Duff had not steered them to an American lawyer in Neuilly they might be waiting to get married still. The lawyer escorted them through the corridors of power and cranked up the sluggish machinery of state—by what means, Paul never knew. He swore before the officials of the U.S. embassy that Paul was who he said he was and had always been; he stood beside Sylvie when she was obliged to swear she was not now and never had been a Communist. He used the telephone the way Duff did, told underlings to connect him with the *chef du bureau*—and said this in such an emphatic way the *chef du bureau* invariably came on.

Finally the separate pieces of paper filled the dossier, in chronological order, with all the necessary seals, *tampons* and signatures intact; the banns were published and the date was set. Paul and Sylvie stood before the mayor in an assembly line ceremony—with five other couples (the oldest named Lejeune)—repeating their *oui*'s in turn to each binding article of the Code Napoléon. The mayor wore a tricolor sash from shoulder to waist and a tricolor ribbon in his buttonhole. Paul did not completely understand the elaborate French vows he had taken, so when he signed his name next to Sylvie's in the massive ledger at the mairie, he pledged again—in a whisper, to his bride—his life and love and meager fortune. To Paul that signing was an act as awesome as birth and death, a moment as solemn as an amen.

Madame Chaix sent them a check for one thousand Swiss francs and the key to her apartment on the Belgian coast. Duff was in Hong Kong, but his secretary came to the flat with the gold cigarette lighters and a magnum of Pommeroy '58.

Paul suddenly remembered their first car: he saw it out there in the middle distance, parked in space, the Renault 4L, with sprigs of lace attached to the radio antenna and the handles of the door.

A cocker spaniel pup clawing at a pet shop window moved Paul to call Sylvie and ask if he could buy the dog for J-P. "No," said Sylvie. (A dumb idea, thought Paul—she's right.) Instead he sent a copy of *Les Adventures de Huckleberry Finn* to his son. Then he bought a set of Napoleonic lead soldiers in an antique shop: he would take them to J-P on Wednesday; meanwhile he arranged the martial figures on his mantelpiece, under the painting by Paul Klee.

Wednesday he rented a car at the Hertz garage in Monte Carlo, but in his haste forgot to bring along the soldiers. He was already at Mouans-Sartoux, halfway to Ys, when he remembered. Next time, then.

The house was out of bounds: it was truly her house now, so they met at the Toison d'Or. J-P came running across the *pré* to greet him, exuberant, affectionate as always. Sylvie sat at a table outside the café and accepted a kiss on one cheek, for form's sake, for she was with a woman friend. The friend was *une femme d'un certain age*, as the French so delicately expressed middle age and beyond; she had remarkably large teeth, but there was no smile to her. She simply showed her teeth and took Paul's hand when they were introduced.

"Maître Beausoleil, *mon mari*," said Sylvie, with a businesslike gesture from one to the other.

"*Enchanté*," said Paul, who was not.

Maître? Paul did not know what the title meant. J-P's schoolteacher was a maître—wasn't a maître always a man? Maître Beausoleil was bareheaded, her rust-colored hair cut short and turning gray under the rust. Sylvie's opposite number—even their perfumes clashed. (And Sylvie was wearing a hat, a wide-brimmed straw hat Paul had not seen for several summers, a perfect frame for his wife's perfect face.) Paul thought of Master B with her crisp professional air and no-nonsense coiffure as perhaps a reincarnation of that long-ago woman psychoanalyst who had so bedeviled Sylvie's adolescence.

Paul borrowed *boules* from Georges, the café owner, and

played *pétanque* with J-P while the ladies sat over tea. The village green lay between the boules court and the café table, and from this distance Paul could not hear what his wife and her friend were saying—but he could see them through the trees, locked in intimate conference. Sylvie's presence was disturbing in an inexplicable way. Even with his back turned Paul felt her there.

To J-P he babbled about a book of Zen that explained how an arrow "shoots itself" when the archer achieves perfect control by clearing his mind of mundane thoughts. Maybe, he suggested to his son, that was the way to play *boules:* Zen and the art of *pétanque.* J-P took this in, wide-eyed and uncomprehending, yet memorizing—as he always did—his father's odd information. When J-P took his turn at *boules* he knocked Papa's winning ball out of the court by pure Provençal skill—no Zen to it.

Mundane thoughts. Paul could not clear his mind, could not concentrate on the game. He kept looking up from the court to that table shaded by a vast linden where Maître Beausoleil held forth and Sylvie listened. Of Sylvie he had only the profile. Still, it was a delight when the breeze nudged his wife's hat brim and her lovely arm went up to hold the hat in place. The disturbing part was that he could see Master B's teeth from here.

"It is your turn to *pointer,* Papa."

Paul sent his *boule* rolling toward the *cochonnet,* then looked up again.

How intently she listens. Had she ever listened with such passion to him? Once upon a time, yes. Sylvie's face (what he could see of it) was alive to whatever her animated friend was explaining; the cup never touched her lips, her tea would turn cold from listening. Once, and only for a moment, she turned his way—but not to look at him, only to indicate her husband, to refer to him to the maître.

That was when Paul abruptly left the game and started walking across the pré. Was it an accumulation of bile or simply a sleepwalker's impulse that set him off? Afterward he would never be able to piece together the rationale that prompted him to abandon his son and stalk menacingly toward his wife. It was an unaccountable act; for once he was a creature of pure instinct, acting out of predetermination, historical necessity, or panic or fury.

"Sylvie!" he called out, still walking toward her. "I want my will back."

She had not heard his approach, and for a moment she was taken by surprise. Her fright gave him a temporary edge; she replied in English.

"Your what?"

The word *will* had come to him out of the *Midi* blue. Why *will*? The thought had taken over, without a drink to sustain it: a solo operation, like the visions of Christine.

"I want my will back."

Maître Beausoleil was startled too. Her flow of French diminished to a murmur.

"Pardon?"

"My will," he said to both of them. He was out of breath from exploding into words after the brisk walk.

"What will?" Sylvie was genuinely puzzled, still taken aback.

"My will I left behind. I gave you."

"You're being very rude," said Sylvie, suddenly recovered and dangerous.

Paul's fists were clenched tight. He made a conscious effort to relax his hands, but he was carrying a *boule* in one of them. He did lower his tone.

"Listen, you sleep with my will under your pillow and it keeps me from sleeping."

"*Tu es fou.*"

Yes I am, thought Paul, but thinking it—the reverse of a Cartesian premise—meant he was not. It occurred to him Sylvie was confusing will with will. Which of course sounded insane. Or did it? Am I out of my mind to want my mind out from under my wife's pillow?

"My testament, I mean. My last will and testament."

This she could deal with, so Sylvie became crisp.

"Maître Beausoleil does not understand English."

"Tough for her. I'm talking to you."

"Your testament is not under my pillow."

"In your drawer, then. Next to the bed."

"So you go through my things."

"My things."

"In my house."

"It's your house but my will."

"If you think—"

"I think I want my will back."

She flushed. She took hold of her hat again, though there was no breeze now. He had never spoken to her in this determined way. She was visibly seeking a tactic, a way to disarm him, so she turned to Maître Beausoleil, translating her husband's ridiculous demand.

"*Son testament?*" said the older woman. "But your copy of his testament is invalid if he should but write another."

So that was what *maître* meant.

"*Il est fou,*" said Sylvie. By averting her eyes and speaking French she seemed to think she had effectively excluded him.

"I am not crazy and I want it back."

"*Ça suffit!*" she snapped.

If there had only been a cutting edge, a blunt instrument

—but there were only teaspoons on the table. He felt the weight of the *boule* for the first time as he struck the table with it, rattling the tea things and his wife.

Maître Beausoleil, rattled too, asked Sylvie: "Shall I call the garçon?"

"*Il n'y en a pas,*" said Paul smiling, calm. "There's only Georges."

"*Vous voyez,*" said Sylvie with a shudder. "You see?" She was offering her husband's behavior as evidence of what they must have discussed before.

The maître was not as steadfast a defender as she first appeared. She had paled at spilled teacups and was wilting now. This was not the way it went in court. When Paul took a breath and turned her way, as if for a fresh assault, she scurried from the table in search of Georges.

"You just lost your professional witness."

"I despise you," said Sylvie, her eyes bright with truth and tears.

"Good," said Paul, relieved. If he had not got that out of her the effort would have been wasted. "Good, I'm glad."

A breeze came up and this time, distracted, Sylvie lost her hat. Strangely enough Paul might have chased the spinning strawpiece across the *pré*, and brought it to her— the last ironic act of a civilized man—but at the same instant he caught sight of J-P struggling up the grassy slope trying to carry five iron *boules* in his arms. All venom drained, his victory turned sour as he stared at the replica of Sylvie and himself: the boy, their essence, the key to all of this, the heart of it, the only thing he wanted from her now and perhaps all along. He ran to his son instead.

Twenty-three

A thin blue stream of cigarette smoke rose through the cannis into a micocoulier tree. Fish was down there. It was his sun trap, in a corner of the garden beyond the rabbit hutches: a three-sided shed of cannis where the sisters stored clay flower pots, last year's bean poles and stacks of carefully folded, empty, plastic fertilizer bags. Fish did not mind the faint clinging smell of fertilizer that lingered in the shed. He spent his mornings there, facing south to store up heat, with his heavy coat (it was June) over his shoulders, smoking cheap cigarettes in an expensive holder. Having avoided the old man all these weeks, Paul now tried to think of an excuse to talk with him.

A bleak morning (all the more so for the relentless sunshine), and no way to kill it. For an hour Paul had folded and stacked his laundry with the meticulous compulsion of an obsessed housewife, then buffed the bottoms of two casseroles with Ajax until he thought he would wear the metal through. He arranged and rearranged the battle line of lead soldiers on the mantelpiece (what spendidly detailed miniature warriors they were) until it seemed they would come alive.

On the balcony he thought maybe Christine would appear, and this time speak. He had to say something to somebody in English. He watched the smoke a moment: he remembered Fish could not afford a newspaper of his own (he borrowed *Nice-Matin* from the Mazarin sisters—only one of whom could read—so as to work out each day's hippodrome winners). Paul rolled up yesterday's *Herald-Tribune* and went down into the garden with it.

Fish was slumped sunwards in a swayback raffia chair—

more turtle than fish—asleep, dreaming perhaps of Rubens and race horses. Paul envied him his insouciant peace. It took a certain mental equilibrium to doze under so many swords of Damocles—garden shears, scythes and spare lawn-mower blades dangled dangerously overhead. There was a still-burning cigarette (the old man would cremate himself someday), but this time, luckily, the Gauloise Bleue had fallen into a flower pot. Paul stubbed it out, lay the newspaper across the old man's lap and left. He would not wake him for the world.

The balcony was a sun trap of Paul's own. My routine, he thought, is no less tedious and time killing than my neighbor's. The mail would come any minute now, by motorbike; then he could pore over the publicity for thermal underwear and debate whether or not to order a complete set of the works of Maupassant. Will I, he asked himself, become another Fish in forty years?

The little radio was no help: somebody had composed a Space Cantata for the astronauts, and France-Musique was playing it. He switched to the news and heard St. Etienne had won the coupe d'Europe, but when the fans mobbed the team's private plane one enthusiast was decapitated by the propeller. This was grim news enough, and he was about to switch it off, but listened through the report of a Swedish physician who had discovered—by weighing a human body before and after death—that the soul weighs twenty grams. It was something he could pass on to J-P one of these days.

He glanced at the page in the typewriter: "The tourists of today should be prepared to—" He walked away from it, then came back and typed the words, "go under."

The mail came. There was a bill from Hertz and a letter (*recommandé*—he had to sign for it) from Sylvie. The letter was no letter, no message inside: just a folded photo-stat, the sight of which gave Paul the bends. It was his will. Seeing those wishes in death signed at the consulate, repro-duced by ghostly Xerox, left him too weak and wasted to come up for air.

Sylvie, he could have sworn, was sitting on the balcony wearing that same hat.

"What about my son?" asked Paul.

"He will, *bien sûr*, remain with me."

"What does he say about that?"

"I do not intend to discuss our situation with a seven-year-old."

Someone from the garden said, "Mr. Swanson, sir."

She was a sealed envelope, cool and white, containing his last will and testament.

"I'm still his father."

"The matter will be settled by *procés*."

"Mr. Swanson?"

She was holding her hat against the wind, and this time it stayed in place.

"What about us, what about me?"

"That is no longer my concern."

"Are you there, Mr. Swanson?"

"When can I see J-P again?"

"*Au tribunal.*"

"Let's speak English, if you don't mind."

"In court."

"He's still my son."

"Excuse me?" said the voice.

"In court," repeated Sylvie, as if the law had the last word on life and death and love.

Paul blinked, then shook his head as if to dislodge the thought. When he looked into the garden Fish was standing below the balcony staring up at him.

"Are you alone?" asked Fish.

"No. I mean yes. Sorry. Talking to myself."

"A taxi has come. With a young man in white. Says his name is Swanson."

"I'm Swanson," said Paul.

"But so is he."

Twenty-four

The two brothers sat on the narrow balcony looking out over a jigsaw puzzle of tile rooftops, olive trees, terraces of artichokes and a long steep walkway lined with cypresses to the sea. The sailor tilted his white hat forward against the glare from the greenhouses of carnations.

"Nice to look at, but why so high up?"

"I like it up here," said Paul. His brother knew nothing about Paul's fear of heights.

"I'd've stayed home and slapped some sense in her head. Your own house—"

"*Our* house." Her house, reflected Paul, really.

"And she kicks you out of it."

"Nobody kicked anybody out. It's called a trial separation."

Only minutes ago when his brother stepped out of the cab from Monte Carlo—in blinding summer whites, wearing that cocky sailor hat on the back of his head—a sudden unexpected joy broke through the miasma of gloom that had plagued Paul all morning. The first delight turned gradually to dismay. (A good thing he had said nothing about how bad things really were.) Paul was beginning to know what the black eagle on Neal's sleeve was all about: it was a bird of prey.

Abruptly Paul asked, "How much time have you got?"

"Till midnight. Cinderella liberty. Like an idiot I wasted all morning looking for your house in Ice."

"Ys. Like 'peace.' "

"Yeah. Ys, Jesus. Old guys in baggy blue denims sitting around whittling sticks. Cemetery full of crooked tombstones, city hall falling in—your bakery don't even wrap the bread up. I walked all the way down a hill behind a bunch of sheep and got sheep shit on my dress shoes."

Neal crossed his legs and inspected the bottom of one shoe.

"What did Sylvie say?" Paul knew she would say nothing about the separation—not to Neal, anyway.

"Said you're staying over here temporarily in Roquebrune —she never said why. Naturally she was surprised to see me. Who expects their long lost brother-in-law they never met to pop up out of nowhere, in Ice?"

"What did you think of Jean-Paul?"

"He talks English with a foreign accent for Christsake. Sylvie told him I'm his uncle from America and he gave me a kiss. Hey, guess what I brought the kid from Naples—a bayonet, a real one."

"A bayonet?"

"You can get anything in Naples. The trick is to get it back to the ship before they can steal it off of you again."

"A bayonet?"

"You can get anything. I traded some dago a gallon of red lead and got this bayonet off him. From one World War or the other, I don't know which, rusty as hell—but a machinist mate buddy of mine polished it up like new. Your kid went ape for it."

Paul could picture J-P's solemn face as he accepted the bayonet from his American uncle.

"I gave Sylvie a picture of the ship. Framed and all."

Paul could see Sylvie's face, too. He got up to bring a bottle of Ricard from the kitchen. He poured for Neal and watered his pastis until the amber liquid turned a clouded yellow, then watered his own. Neal made a face when he tasted it.

"This all you got to drink?"

"There's a bar in Monte Carlo I go to where they know how to make martinis."

"France," said Neal. "Drinks that taste like licorice, no wrappers on the bread. It's the fucking Dark Ages over here. No wonder France never won a war since Napoleon."

"It's better with ice. But I've got no refrigerator."

"That's what I mean."

"I'll buy you a martini, in Monte Carlo."

Neal stared hard at his brother, squinting, as if he could see inside his skull: "When you going to cut the shit and come home?"

"This is home. Ys, I mean. Where the hell's your home— a ship?"

"Right. An American ship. And nobody going to kick me off it."

"Nobody kicked anybody. It's a trial separation."

"Yeah. That's what they call it."

"We're trying to work things out."

"What's to work out? She's got you sweating it out over here in the doghouse drinking licorice. I'd've stayed home and slapped some sense in her head. You think on account of she was born over here she's too high class to slap around? They're all alike, believe me. Try being nice and it gets you nowhere. Patty was the same way. Give them an inch and they'll cut your balls off. Patty tried getting smart with me and I knocked her on her ass."

Paul knew, but asked anyway, "Where did that get you?"

"Nowhere, either—but it was a hell of a satisfaction at the time."

With the remembered satisfaction on his face, Neal settled back in the canvas chair. Recalling that happy event so distracted him he took a careless sip of the pastis, then screwed up his face.

"How can you drink this stuff?"

"You get used to it."

"Yeah, but *why?* Want to know what your trouble is?"

"No," said Paul.

"Your trouble is, you dump your own country to go live in France and get married to a foreigner, for kicks, and got *used* to it. Now look at you."

Neal's voice was full of the wounds and rivalries from childhood, and Paul would not have been surprised to hear him go into the old argument over who really urinated on the toilet seat both of them got punished for.

"Look at yourself." Paul stared pointedly at the light blue four-leaf clover tattooed on Neal's forearm: PATTY (his ex-wife, in capital letters), with *Cheryl* and *Dyane* (in script)— each name framed in a separate leaf, the fourth leaf blank.

"So what?" said Neal, looking at the tattoo with distaste. "I know a guy on East Main in Norfolk that takes these things off."

"What about your kids?"

"She got the kids and I got my freedom."

The word made Paul dizzy, and he put his drink down.

That was a word you shouldn't bring up, drinking. Paul steadied himself in the fragile sling of pegs and canvas. The balcony was going out from under him. Before he plummeted Paul searched the garden for a fleeting, sustaining glimpse of Christine. He did not quite fall. The comforting ghost was nowhere in sight; but he knew she was there, and this was what held the balcony up, held the world together.

Neal, meanwhile, stared into the murky depths of the drink he despised. He looked as unhappy as Paul felt—but he quickly recovered himself, threw the pastis over the balcony railing and said, "Hey, what about that bar you were talking about?"

"It's in Monte Carlo. There's a bus in about an hour."

"What do you mean, bus?"

"Sylvie's got the car."

"You mean she's got your car?"

"Our car." (Paid for by his mother-in-law—something else not to go into with Neal.) "She has to shop, she has to take Jean-Paul to school."

But the outrage was worse than anything Neal had heard so far. He slammed down the empty glass so hard it cracked, then fell apart. "Jesus, if she was my wife . . . "

Paul picked up the shards of glass and carried them inside, glad to be out of his brother's range for a moment. When he came back Neal was checking his hand for cuts, staring into his open palm as if—it seemed to Paul—he was trying to read his fortune there.

"I should've kept the cab. We could've gone back down in the cab."

Suddenly Neal was rummaging in his canvas bag, fumbling among the scattered packs of duty-free cigarettes to bring up what looked like a life-size toy. It was no toy. At the sight of it Paul swallowed hard, his breath caught.

"What's the matter? It ain't loaded." Neal placed the revolver on the low table between them. He dug down into his bag again and brought out a clip of cartridges. "I carry the clip separate, to play it safe."

"Where did you get that thing?"

"Naples. You can get anything in Naples."

"But what for?"

"I always wanted a Beretta. But I'd never be able to get it back to the States. Everybody's uptight about drugs coming in. I was on shore patrol when I bought it and the guy I was on shore patrol with warned me they pull a surprise locker inspection out at sea, my ass's in a sling."

Paul had edged his deck chair away from the table, but he could not keep his eyes from the deadly blue-black weapon.

"The shells for it are .38's," said Neal, tossing the clip onto the table beside the Beretta. "You can get them anyplace."

Paul looked out to sea to still his heartbeat. Corsica was there behind the horizon, just out of sight. He had an urge to sail to Corsica, an island full of butterflies.

"Mom says you stopped writing lately."

"Things the way they are, I didn't want to write. How is she?"

"The same. Worse. She sits around all the time knitting. Her varicose veins are so bad she can hardly stand up."

Paul saw his mother, seated. Sylvie's mother sat knitting beside her. Our mothers knit and wait, thought he.

"I bought her some rubber stockings, but you know her— she won't wear them. I told her to at least put some bandages on her legs for Christsake, but all she did was call in a practitioner and they sat around and prayed together. Mom's living in a dream world, like you."

When they left Neal put the pistol back in the canvas bag,

and he carried the bag with him—but Paul knew the sleek instrument was meant for himself, it was his brother's idea of a gift.

Twenty-five

The painting above the bar was a copy of Gauguin's *D'où venons-nous? Que sommes-nous? Où allons-nous?*

Neal squinted into the fluorescent light that framed the painting: "What does it say?"

"Where do we come from?" said Paul. "What are we? Where are we going?"

"That's a good question."

Chantal brought their drinks to the booth. She seldom served; she always sat at the bar, second stool from the cash register. She was a fixture of the place, as standard as the Gauguin reproduction she sat under—where does she come from? what is she? where is she going?

"*Votre frère?*" she asked as she put down the drinks, two martinis, American style, scrupulously mixed by the Corsican dwarf behind the bar. She spoke warmly to Paul—they were old friends, since the ride back from the hippodrome. But this was the first time she had approached him at the Tahiti Café. She was probably attracted by Neal's uniform; she would know about uniforms. She said: how they resembled one another—could the sailor be his brother?

"What did she say?" asked Neal.

"She said you look like me."

"Ask her who's the best looking."

"*Qu'est-ce qu'il dit?*"

When Paul translated she laughed, delightedly, and put a long tapered nail to her lower lip. She looked from one brother to the other, as if comparing their features. Her face was expressive when she laughed, but her teeth were discolored from nicotine. She wore only enough makeup to outline her lips and eyes under the harsh café lights. Her clothes were discreet and expensive. She was French, after all, and would know how to display herself, prostitute or not.

"*Il est drôle, votre frère.*"

"What did she say?

"She said you're a funny man."

"Tell her I think she's cute. Ask her to sit down and have a drink."

Neal made room for her on his side of the booth, and Chantal sat with him. She made a signal and the Corsican came over immediately with a *vin blanc-cassis*. With the pale drink before her and a place secured at the booth (a dinghy, loosely moored to a larger ship), Chantal lapsed into the somber reserve of the waiting game. It is a game we all play, thought Paul. You put in all that time waiting for something to happen to heal a marriage, but nothing happens. Meanwhile your wife waits for you to give up waiting—and if you won't be reasonable, and quit, she ends it. The fate of waiters.

Neal played the game from another angle: not the passive, patient role, but the waiter with time to kill. (He was at sea level now, and sure of himself.) He had established a promising beachhead on the shores of Monaco and could afford to wait.

Waiting, too, for his final six-year hitch to pass: he would retire from the Navy before he was forty.

"I'll make Chief before then." He went on talking to Paul as if the girl were not there. "I'm set for life," he said, for the second time, and Paul looked away. "How about you? Last time I heard, you was going great guns."

Paul got quickly into his drink.

"Mutual funds, wasn't it?"

"Right. That, and other things." The drink helped. He had gone too long without a decent drink. But the U.S. eagle was about to pounce.

"What happened?"

"It was a company called Amazing Growth that suddenly stopped growing."

"How come?"

He would do his imitation of Duff: "The late Sixties were bad times for offshore funds. Market was bearish. Company overextended. Poor performance three quarters in a row, with redemptions running higher than sales. Swiss authorities stepped in, little men with brief cases began asking questions."

Paul half expected his cigarette to explode.

"That stuff's over my head."

"Over mine, too. I was still grinding out glowing publicity the day A.G. went into receivership."

"So you went under?"

"Right. Glug, glug. Over everybody's head." (Except Duff's. Captains of conglomerates do not go down with the ship.)

"You was going great guns, last I heard."

"I was paid a salary commensurate with the superlatives I employed."

"What's that supposed to mean?" A mistake to try to snow Neal with words. He turned to Chantal and said, "Now he don't even have a car."

Paul translated and Chantal nodded: she remembered picking up Paul at the race track, she knew how these things went. Once one had a car, it was *malheureux* to be without. Paul fumbled in his pocket for the extra set of car keys he still carried. There was a rabbit's foot attached to the key chain, for luck.

"Know something," said Neal, indicating Chantal with his thumb, "a different hair style and she'd look just like Sylvie."

"She doesn't look anything like Sylvie."

The drink hurt, going down, as he said her name. I will have to take time off, thought he, from feeling sorry for myself. I will stiffen my upper lip, go into my Rowland Thompson routine, and float through this glorious day with baby brother.

"The hair's different—but she looks like her to me."

"Not to me."

From the angle of Neal's thumb Chantal knew she was being discussed. She tilted her head slightly, posing for a photograph. Neal's free hand on Chantal's side dropped below the level of the table—while Paul turned away, and pretended to read the fly-specked articles of the *Répression de l'Ivresse Publique.*

"I mean, like you was supposed to be the Big Brain in the family."

"Now I'm the last pedestrian."

"I didn't even go to college."

"You didn't miss much."

"I could've been an ensign by now, if I'd've went to college."

As Paul drained the last swallow of martini it occurred to him he could not pay for the drinks.

"Listen, Lad, I just remembered. I don't have any money."

"No kidding?" Neal was not just sympathetic—he was delighted to hear. He shifted his hand from Cantal's thigh to the billfold tucked into his tight sailor pants. "I only got about fifty on me, but I can get some more off a guy on the ship. You really tap city? Hey, I'll take you back to

Villefranche with me tonight and get some bread off this guy I know."

Neal sucked in his stomach, pried the billfold from his belt and slapped it on the table.

"Count it," he said happily.

Chantal purred softly at the sight of new green. She leaned forward as Paul counted twelve crisp fives.

"Take forty for now till I see Pike and borrow some."

"Have you got any French money?"

"What's wrong with dollars?"

"Nothing. Only we can't pay for the drinks with dollars. Banks are closed till two-thirty."

"France, Jesus."

Chantal knew there was a problem involving currency. She offered to exchange the dollars at the official rate, if Neal wanted to come with her.

"What did she say?"

"She said she's got some money upstairs. She'll change your dollars for you, if you want."

"Can I trust her?"

"For that, yes."

The booth, with no one in it but himself, turned out to be a tomb. He kept trying to swallow an unpleasant aftertaste; he could not get enough air. It was that dead interval between lunch and the apéritif hour, and Neal was still somewhere with Chantal. The droplets of sweat on the backs of his hands made him think of the beaded moisture on the outside of a martini glass, so he ordered another.

Meanwhile the café had filled with le troisième age, the French for "senior citizens": elderly ladies with parchment skin and stiffly curled blue-gray hair; old men in suits far too heavy for the Mediterranean seaside. There were canes hooked to the backs of chairs. When one stiff gentleman bent to kiss the back of a hand between the ruff of a lace glove and a wristwatch, Paul imagined he could hear bones snap. They still do that, thought he, the kissing of hands. It was like watching a silent film.

Except for his booth, and the treacherous bar stools, the café was filled. Each time his respiration stalled, he looked for a fire exit, for a way out. Claustrophobia was new to him. Put it on the list, thought Paul, add it to the bill. Until the martini arrived he thought he would never catch his breath.

They might as well have waited here—the banks and *bureaux de changes* would be open now. Of course currency exchange was not what the transaction was all about. You put them together, he reminded himself—what did you expect? The deformed barman was watching the clock too, but coolly; he was accustomed to it. For that little while there was a bond between Paul and the dwarf: they were playing the waiting game together. In fact, the waiting game was being played on all sides: the elderly retired waiting to die.

Paul tried to think his way out of the thought of death, to savor his drink and what was left of the afternoon. Instead of the big death, think about the little one, *la petite morte*. Would he rather have gone to spill himself into her than wait for Neal to do it?

There was a joke here, but it would be blasphemous to laugh. (No laughter in the presence of the living dead.) He and Sylvie, with two expressive languages in common and ten years of shared intimacy to call on, could not communicate on any level—certainly not the horizontal, where two unmatched strangers like Neal and Chantal could come colliding together with no need of words. Maybe his brother was right, about all of it. You controlled the situation with pure primal thrust.

There was a stir of life in the wax museum: the old people were suddenly animated. They looked up from their espresso cups and cognac snifters as Chantal came clicking down the wrought-iron spiral staircase in her stiletto heels. Her skirt was aswirl like a gypsy's, and Neal—touching those two sacred bulges: adjusting his crotch, caressing his wallet—followed closely behind the skirt, an idiot grin of success on his face. Several of the old men smiled in return. One old fellow who looked like Fish, with a *legion d'honneur* ribbon in his buttonhole, contentedly cocked his head, happy at this underside view of Chantal's legs. However, in the face of the Corsican dwarf Paul recognized something closer to pain than applause at the performance on the staircase.

"Guess what?" said Neal when he got to the table. "She's got a car."

"I know," said the last pedestrian.

Twenty-six

The boulevard leading out of town was as surgically scoured as a hospital corridor. Are there any cleaner gutters in all the world? (The Monagesque street cleaners were ghosts too—they swept at night.) It had rained just long enough to bring up a mist along the shore, but the center of Monte Carlo was all bright surface in the hard light of late afternoon, no hint of dust. The cornices of banks had been set by micrometer, the paving stones polished by hand—it was like passing one long window display by Cartier.

Mist obliterated the grotesque hotel perched on the nose of the Tête de Chien, but Paul could make out the canti-levered chateau that marked the village of Roquebrune floating insubstantially above their heads. Traveling west, he felt he was saying goodbye to the place.

Like a thick coil of hawser, Neal was curled up in the back seat; he snored delicately in his sleep, the little canvas bag under one ear. Three martinis had mellowed Paul just enough to blunt the words, "I despise you," but not elimi-nate the threat. Chantal was talking about men and dogs. Veils of mist floated across the Grande Corniche, the same misty ribbons that floated across Paul's mind.

Chantal might know the patchwork roadway by heart, but what if the speeding red car veered sharply to the left, and smashed the barrier? Paul pictured the Fiat spinning bumper over bumper along the sheer cliffside to the sea. For a little while he toyed with that heart-stopping possibility, but sleepily. He could see Sylvie's stricken face vividly enough when she came to identify the crushed body on the rocks of Cap d'Ail, and he could create the *mise en scène* of searchlights and grappling hooks, but he could not make it to the *pompes funèbres* with himself as centerpiece, in a long pine box. No, he was unable to carry the vision as far as graveside—anyway, Chantal was chattering about what she wanted out of life.

"The man I want I think is like you."

"You mean, like my brother."

"Ah, your brother is *drôle* indeed. To marry, not so *drôle*."

She wanted *un mari* who was *un vrai mari*—no more Monte Carlo studs for her. She was weary of the *snobisme* around here. *Tout le monde veut en profiter de moi.* She had had it up to here (she put a finger under her chin); she would prefer to live in a trailer on the crowded beach at

Sète. She would prepare *steak-frites* for her *vrai mari* on a butane gas stove, like all the world.

I'm a husband all right, thought Paul, an endangered species. Chantal knows a rare bird when she sees one: the last of the wife lovers, the last truly married man. Why didn't I marry a whore and live in a trailer and eat steak and French fries on the beach at Sète?

He looked down at the rocks and nearly fainted from nausea and vertigo.

She could not keep a dog in her flat above the Tahiti Café, but when she married they would have a dog called Whiskey —unless her husband chose another name. Paul casually reminded her she would become a minor, completely dependent on her husband under the Code Civil. Had she thought of that?

"I *want* to be dependent. He may sign everything, *mon mari.*"

Could a man ever truly know a woman's mind? As he sat beside this prostitute plunging down a mist-covered road while she invented her life and made up her marriage from scratch, he had encountered the perpetual mystery again, in a different setting.

The dog she wanted was a miniature poodle, unless her husband wanted another kind. Paul was about to tell her she could not even work without her husband's permission— when he remembered what her work was.

Instead he asked, "Will you have room enough in a trailer for children?"

The car swerved slightly, but they made the curve. Anyway, thought Paul, I've got my blood type in my billfold.

"*Les enfants?*" She was perplexed. He had broken into her dream with that thought, but she picked it up again. Maybe they would have two poodles, one called Whiskey, one called Coco.

This is the way we marry, thought Paul—like plunging off a cliff.

"We would have to get a larger car than this one, to pull a trailer from Monaco to Sète."

Twenty-seven

Neal was drinking cognac (and asked Paul to ask the waiter "to put some ice in it, for the love of Christ,")—at the same time pointing out his ship, the A.P.A. Cayuga, attack transport, anchored in the unlikely vicinity of a sleekly varnished three-masted schooner. The *Cayuga* lay like a scrap heap dumped into the shadowy bluegreen waters of the bay, top-heavy with booms and winches—a vague embarrassment, to Paul's uncertain eye—with its jagged streak of rust-proofing red lead along the waterline like a strip of dirty underwear showing.

They were seated on the terrace of an "American bar" in Villefranche, but Paul was vague about when or how they got there. The terrace overlooked the bay along Cap Ferrat, and to the west, the stony precincts of the Citadelle. The late sun (how did it get so late so early?) lighted the edges of the Citadelle ramparts and cast deep shadows across the quai. There was a breeze now, and it rippled the flat white collars of the sailors coming ashore. The perspiration on Paul's forehead began to dry in the fresh breeze; his hands were steadier, but slightly numb. Somewhere between Monte Carlo and Villefranche he had got dizzy from looking at the rocks, then sick, and he had vomited the *choucroute* from lunch (the dwarf must have poisoned him, purposely), but he had thoughtfully got out of Chantal's car to do so. There was a bell-shaped glass in front of him, with *eau de vie* in it, but it seemed safer not to touch it.

Raspoutine was still with them, but without the cat. Paul wondered fuzzily what became of the Siamese cat that traveled on Raspoutine's shoulder and what his brother thought of Chantal's ink-stained friend with the Castro beard they had picked up at his atelier under the arcades. His breath smelled of vinegary supermarket *rouge* as he talked through his wet beard about the new series of erotic engravings he hoped to sell to the sailors of the Sixth Fleet. Paul remembered sitting on a horse blanket of cat hairs and possibly the dried stains of lovemaking, spread beside Raspoutine's flatbed printing press, while the liter of Préfontaine went around. Neal had remained standing, suspicious of the scroungy blanket, scratching at his crotch and studying the ink and watercolor prints (a tangle of lovers taken from the Kama-Sutra, or the backs of Pigalle playing cards) strung along a wire above the press, to dry. The window of Raspoutine's shop displayed only calling cards and menus and a single stock copy of a catechism he printed for the local priest, as camouflage. He printed at night, for he had no commercial license.

"*Je suis libre,*" he declared. He had no working papers, no *carte d'identité;* he had fled the military service in Switzerland. He wore no uniform, he paid no taxes.

"What's he saying?" asked Neal.

"He's free. He doesn't have to carry any I.D."

"*Il est artiste,*" explained Chantal.

"He looks like a fuckup to me."

From their table they could study the grotesque lines of

the *Cayuga* in repose. Paul watched the flatnosed liberty boats make their swerving run from the *Cayuga* to the Gare Maritime, where a temporary USO shed had been set up to change dollars into francs and distribute tourist maps of downtown Nice to the visiting American sailors. It hurt Paul's eyes to look too hard at the white uniforms in the late sun, but Neal checked out each new arrival with a squint of inspection and seemed to glow in the growing presence of his own ship's company. The tables on the terrace began to fill with uniforms. The Navy men sat quietly at first; they trickled in by boarding parties of two and three, self-consciously American in a foreign place. Then, as the terrace became crowded with their own, their voices mounted, they tilted chairs back against the bulkhead, or the terrace railing, drank too quickly and called for "Encore!" They liked the word *encore* and perhaps drank up, double time, just to be able to say it. The most recently arrived came aboard with considerable swagger: these were Neal's own deck force, and they pulled a table up to his. A round of drinks—"*Encore!*" —for their bosun's mate and his civilian friends. While the drinks were on the way they openly appraised and obliquely lusted after the lady at Neal's side.

Now there were two bell-shaped glasses in front of Paul. He made a careless gesture and heard a splintering crash.

"Ça alors," said Chantal, startled when Paul's glass was overturned.

Her French so delighted the crew of the *Cayuga* one of them threw his glass to the floor, so that she would say it again.

"Jarhead," said Neal. The sailor who had thrown the glass was not a sailor but a Marine. "We can carry fifteen hundred of the bastards, if we have to."

Some of the spilled *eau de vie* dripped onto Paul's pants.

"What's her name?" a yeoman asked Neal, tilting his beer bottle in Chantal's direction, and Neal asked Paul to ask Chantal what her name was. Paul was offended for Chantal to realize his brother did not know the name of the girl he had gone to bed with, and said, in a voice he did not recognize as his own, "The lady's name's her own affair."

"Her name's Sylvie," said Neal.

Paul was ready to fight, if only he could find his legs which had fallen off somewhere below the knees.

"Sylvie's my wife," said Paul, both indignant and hurt.

"She's your wife?" asked the yeoman, meaning Chantal.

"She's *my* wife," said Neal, and the hand on Chantal's side dropped below the level of the table.

The tallest of the sailors gave Chantal a flip salute: two fingers to the brim of his white hat. He could not speak. His nose was stitched across the bridge; there were black and purple bruises under his eyes, and his jaw was wired together in a grin.

"This here is Pike, the guy I told you about," said Neal.

Pike nodded.

The yeoman was Pike's mouthpiece, and explained: "He got dented by a Chianti bottle in a bar in Naples."

"You can get anything," said Paul, "in Naples."

Neal suddenly stretched out his free arm (the other was engaged, the hand on Chantal's thigh), his elbow positioned carefully on the table, his fingers stretched apart: "Drinks are on me," he declared, "if anybody can put me down."

The yeoman with *Tucker* stencilled on his white hat was the first to try. He reached across the table as if to shake Neal's hand; the two men ritually touched palms and locked fingers. Paul blearily studied the tattooed names, upsidedown, on his brother's arm: *Dyane, Cheryl* and finally PATTY, all caps. Paul had his own version of a tattoo—the scar Sylvie had given him, to remember her by—and he reached down as if to touch it, but touched only the sticky liquid from his spilled drink.

Without the least strain showing in his face (it was Tucker's face that showed exertion), Neal swiftly bent the other man's arm backwards until the sleeve with the crossed quills touched the tabletop.

"Fuck," said Tucker—then quickly to Chantal, "Excuse my French."

Chantal applauded delicately, laughed her discreet professional laugh. A potato-faced gunner's mate named Petrotsky tried, but Neal put him down. Williamson went down, as well as Finney. Pike was the last to try, and held up stiffly, longer than any contender so far—but went down, too, with his grin fixed, even in defeat.

Neal offered his arm to Raspoutine, who politely declined. He declined with style, and a smile of *merci*, but thanks no. Then Neal said to Paul, "You want to Indian-wrestle me, big brother?"

"Go wrestle yourself," said Paul cheerfully. "Wrestle her."

Neal, beaming, offered the flat of his hand to Chantal, who playfully put her hand against his. He let her push his forearm backwards, easily, until *Dyane*, *Cheryl* and PATTY were flattened.

"Drinks are on me," Neal crowed.

"You really his brother?" Tucker asked Paul.

"Rowland Thompson's the name."

"He says you're his brother."

"We're divorced," said Paul, "but we're trying to work things out."

A taxi driver—too late for the first assault wave of sailors, too early for the next landing party—pulled up alongside the quay, calling out: "Hey, Marines! You get a nice taxi ride the whole Riviera coastals!" Sailors were throwing peanuts and olive pits at him.

Meanwhile Raspoutine, sitting coolly beside Chantal, played the waiting game with great patience and considerable style. He can afford to wait, mused Paul, he knows her in another language. Tonight, when the Navy shipped out, Raspoutine would get his village back, and the girl. So he sat quietly in the midst of America watching as if from a distance, waiting. The French style: Sylvie had it, so did J-P. Even when Raspoutine got up and strolled across the wooden plank café terrace to the pinball machine (an American device) the sailors watched, for he wore his cool like his corduroy jacket, a cape draped over his shoulder. The ingenious American machine could not defeat him, even if he lost. He was like the cab driver—parked across the street now, out of range of American missiles—polishing one fender where the olive pits hit it, patient, waiting, fixed in time. Time is on their side, concluded Paul, and they know it.

When Raspoutine left the pinball machine, a sailor called out, "Hey, Castro!" but Raspoutine continued on his way with a benevolent smile and blessed the sailor with an upraised hand. Hard to believe Raspoutine and Sylvie came from the same cold country. That's where they get their cool, thought Paul, they have no central heating.

A Chief Engineer who must have been drinking elsewhere came by and said, "This is the life, who's the lady?"

"Lady's name's her own affair," said Neal, not looking up. The Chief went off to sit down heavily at an empty table.

"Snipes," said Tucker, meaning engineers. "They got no fucking diplomacy."

A seaman apprentice known as Tender Gear wanted to call home, but Petrotsky told him the time stateside wasn't the same as here. His momma was no doubt street-walking at this hour. The boy's face was red, the color of peach next to the pale potato face of the gunner's mate. But everybody's face was tinted in the dying light. Liberty boats crisscrossed the flat red surface of the bay like skimming insects on a summer pond; the white uniforms of the seamen coming ashore reflected orange in the *feu d'artifice* of a Mediterranean sunset.

Chantal thought Navy uniforms were *mignons* and Paul translated. The sailors at the table cheered, and Neal put his white hat on Janine's head and called for another round— but the waiter refused to come out on the terrace because somebody had set off a life-raft flare and singed the back of his jacket. Another glass crashed, or was it a bottle?

A jeep pulled up where the cab had been, a jeep the Shore Patrol had ferried over from the *Cayuga* on an LCT.

At the same time Paul was asking Raspoutine, *"Dites-moi, vous êtes Suisse, vraiment?"* Tucker said to Paul, "No kidding, is Boats really your brother?"

Paul could not believe the unwashed printer with the wire-brush beard could come from the same world as Sylvie.

"Once upon a time, yes," said Raspoutine in English, his beard glowing like copper wire ends in the setting sun. "I carry no papers, I am an *illégitime*." But as he said it his cool failed temporarily: he was watching the S.P. warily.

Two Marines from the jeep, in arm bands and brassards, stepped gingerly onto the terrace (a minefield of broken glass by now) and moved in on a radarman with winestains down the front of his jumper. (It was he who had set off the life-raft flare.) As the marines jerked him upright his hat fell off and rolled as far as Paul's shoe: Freeman stenciled on the down-turned brim—another free man. One of the Shore Patrolmen gave Chantal a wink as they coldly stiff-armed Freeman into a side-stepping soft shoe all the way to the jeep.

Something Paul wanted to ask Chantal, something about setting up housekeeping in a trailer—but he could not bring himself to speak to her as long as his brother's hat was on her head and his hand on her thigh.

"I came out ahead," Neal was telling Raspoutine, when he found out Rice Pudding spoke English, and became accustomed to his odor. "My Navy lawyer talked rings around that hick shyster of hers."

Raspoutine knocked his pipe out on a chair leg and told Neal he had left a *femme* behind in Switzerland. Neal wasn't listening, but Paul was. Did Raspoutine mean woman or wife?

"She didn't get shit," said Neal, "except the kids."

Except the kids, Paul thought—but wasn't that everything?

Civilians, with a mission, were making the rounds of the tables. They were sober-looking men and young men in electric blue suits selling bottle-green Bibles.

"*Temoins de Jéhove,*" explained Raspoutine, and Chantal bestowed upon them her most frigid stare. One did not solicit openly like that—it was completely unprofessional.

I could always go into the Bible business, Paul suggested to himself. Remember Farber. Farber, a top salesman with Amazing Growth, became a Witness when the company went under. Switched his faith from one expanding organization to another. Today he was selling Bibles somewhere, instead of mutual funds. Here, the Bibles were selling like *petits pains*, like hotcakes, as souvenirs—because they were in French.

How did these American faces become so incredibly American? Paul recognized every face at every table. No

wonder his fellow citizens came to this "American Bar"—
there were ice cubes, Bibles and a pinball machine. (They
were missing a jukebox, but that would come.) A babel of
Brooklynese and Birmingham washed over him, and Paul
tried to insert himself into the spirit of it, to work up a
homespun nostalgia—but he could not feel anything below
the heart. His feet had gone to sleep and his wrists had
swollen. His wristwatch was a gift from his mother-in-law;
he took it off and put it into his pocket. There was a mark
where his watch had been, like a tattoo. He then assumed
his Phantom Inspector aspect: his face turned instantly to
plaster, his inscrutable smile was wired together exactly like
Pike's. Why no lights, with night coming on? The ashtrays
were overflowing with duty-free cigarette butts. The Phantom
Inspector automatically blackballed from *Grimwald's Guide*
any café owner crude enough to put ice into cognac. He
would deny the place a star, even as the evening star became
visible, and the ship's string of lights flickered on.

A small girl was talking to the waiter. *Ten Nights on a
Barroom Floor:* "Is my father in there?" Christine? Paul's
plaster aspect failed—but just then a troupe of Witnesses
went by: blue suits and green Bibles came between father
and daughter. He tried to get up but his legs were gone.
When the Witnesses passed out of the line of vision he saw
the waiter was not talking to a little girl, but to the *patron*,
a worried man in rimless glasses wondering if it was worth
catering to freespending sailors if it meant a wrecked terrace.
Should have thought of that, Paul wanted to tell him, before
you start calling yourself an "American bar."

Paul missed Christine. He had wanted to see not just a
familiar face, but someone close. Disappointed, he turned
to his brother, but his brother was gone: Neal was hustling.
The sight of money changing hands must have reminded him

his own brother was broke; he had taken his hat back from Chantal and Pike was peeling off banknotes into it. A collection, Neal's hat going around (it went from Petrotsky to Williamson to Finney to Pike), and even though it was Neal's hat, Paul felt a vague shame, a panhandler by proxy. Raspoutine coolly declined. Tender Gear lowered his pants, he kept his money in a money belt. Neal was working this table for his big brother while the Witnesses worked the other tables for Jehovah.

Tucker leaned across the table as if to Indian-wrestle Chantal, and said, "I never kissed a French girl in my life."

Paul translated. Chantal took the cigarette from her lips, smiled and bent far forward to kiss the blue-eyed sailor on both cheeks: *"Voila!"* In the background a quartet of black steward mates sang *When the Saints Go Marching In* as the Jehovah's Witnesses marched off.

Neal spilled the contents of the white hat in front of Paul. "My boys," said he, "are the greatest. Didn't I tell you the *Cayuga'd* come through?"

Chantal's eyes liquefied at the sight of negotiable currency so casually displayed. The tips of her breasts touched green as she bent to inhale the mixed perfume of all that loose cash. Paul fingered a twenty vaguely; he felt like the bank in a Monopoly game. He was American enough to feel American about money: it was printed paper you earned as much of as you could—then got rid of, as quickly as possible. Raspoutine was visibly stirred by the sudden American largesse. While Chantal counted the loot like an eager Casino croupier, Raspoutine examined the bills as works of art: true, they were inferior to the multicolored franc notes, but they did not come apart in your hands. Then he got hold of himself, retired into his cool and watched from a distance, sucking a cold pipe. There is nothing, thought Paul, so superior as a superior Frenchman—but of course Raspoutine wasn't French, he was Swiss.

Now that Neal had purchased his brother's soul, he leaned across Chantal's shoulder to ask: "What's really the matter between you two?"

"Between who? What two?"

"You and your wife."

It was his brother asking, in his brother's keeper's tone. The French would never push their way into a man's private life. But Grimwald, Joan Duff and now Neal all had to have affadavits from him on the state of his marriage.

"Is it sex? If it ain't sex it's got to be money."

Paul studied the twenty in the poor light and could have sworn Hamilton's jaw was wired, like Pike's. If only it was as easy as sex or money, if only it came down to that. Easy come, easy go: money selling stocks or Bibles or words—or easier, out of a sailor's hat. For sex there were specialists— in America, anyway (but they would be over here any day now, selling Sex in France)—who for a fee unraveled the knot of intercourse and restructured the male and female for simultaneous orgasm—or sold you a book that tells how. Put your organs in the hands of experts and count on computers to make it right; meanwhile, if Paul could have pulled his wits together and trusted his numbed tongue he might have attempted a lecture on the difference between sex and love (amour, they called it, locally) with Over There attitudes and Over Here practices, but just then Tender Gear brought his baffled red face back to the table, saying, "There's a lady in charge of the men's room," and said it for him.

"It was I," confessed Paul, "who pissed on the toilet seat when we were kids."

Neal did not hear, or took no notice—all swagger gone, only maudlin reminiscence now—he was trying to tell Paul something about his own shattered marriage; how, in the beginning "I shit you not"—he loved his wife.

A Swiss heart works like clockwork and an American's is all mush, but we manage our loving ceremonies all the same.

"And she loved me," Neal was saying.

Unless she lied. They do that, the ladies—Chantal would, Joan Duff did. But Sylvie's eyes were gray and open—gray as a Swiss lake in winter—and she did not lie with them, at least not with her eyes open.

"I wrote her letters. From everyplace, Lisbon, Panama, Mayaguez. Everytime we went overseas I wrote her a fucking letter."

Neal's schoolboy scrawl could barely cope with Beginning Algebra before he dropped out of school, and now to sign a ship's muster or his own liberty card was probably painful. He was rubbing his tattoo as if he might conjure PATTY up out of the thin blue cloverleaf inscribed on his flesh.

The S.P. jeep was back; they had brought along a megaphone: "Last liberty boat! Last call!" Tender Gear, rebuffed at the WC, was urinating through the *provisoire-définitif* chicken wire railing into the sea. One lone helmeted bruiser rapped on the table top with his billy club: "Last call, you guys!" The sailors began to check themselves for wallet, cigarettes, liberty card, Bible. Paul, under the sway of the military command, checked himself, and found his wristwatch in his pocket.

"You can't trust them," Neal was saying to Paul, and he turned to Raspoutine for confirmation, "Right?" But Raspoutine, at the sight of the shore patrol, drew himself deeper into his empty pipe.

The string of deck lights around the terrace came on at last and the waiter shuffled forward in the mournful spirit of "Going Home," the spiritual the steward mates were singing.

He was trying to collect whatever money the sailors might have left after the Witnesses. We spread some green around, thought Paul, and tip our hats to the ladies. The Chief Engineer came by, tipped his visor to Chantal and fell flat on his face. We come here in landing parties, on assignment, on tour—to fuck Europe, as Neal put it.

"I saved up for her," Neal was saying, but Paul could not hear what he saved up—sex or money—for the night stick drumming on the table and "Going Home."

Two snipes shifted the Bibles they had bought, picked up the Chief Engineer by the shoulders and dragged him through the splinters of glass to the quay. The lights flattered Chantal's face, and she accepted the sidelong glances of homage from departing sailors, with lowered eyes. Raspoutine had got his pipe lit and was shaking Neal's hand goodbye and drinking the last of Paul's *eau de vie*. A quartermaster said the fucking tide was coming up, but his buddy told him his fucking socks were soaked with beer.

Now that he was leaving, Tucker said, "No kidding," one last time: "You guys actually brothers?"

Behind Chantal's back Paul and Neal leaned close—as close as they had ever been—and Paul pushed beyond the pile of Monopoly money to lean closer. He tried to say something, anything, to the brother whose forehead nearly touched his own, but it was Neal who spoke: "With Patty and me, I admit, it was sex. What about you?"

"I'll call Sylvie and find out."

Twenty-eight

Paul was surprised to find his feet where he left them. Easy does it, watch the glass. He got up and went into the café to ask the girl at the cash register if he might make a call. As he gave her the number he practiced perfect speech control in preparation for the conversation with his wife. It would not do to let Sylvie hear, and draw conclusions from, any trace of alcohol in his voice. He had to hear her say something besides "I despise you"—something even more final than that. What about the vows in Paris, what about four thousand nights? From his end he would simply present his sane and balanced self for her to deal with.

"*Ne quittez pas,*" said the cashier after she had dialed and got a response. She handed him the telephone.

"Sylvie?"

"*Allo?*"

At first he could not believe the voice at the other end. His hand (the one that held the receiver) went cold, and the cold passed through his arm to pierce his heart. *If a man answers hang up,* went the jingle. A man had answered; Paul hung up.

A mistake, surely. Another failing of the French telephone service—or the girl had dialed incorrectly. He might have given her the wrong number: even after ten years in France Paul still stumbled over those digits composed of multiples of twenty, the *quatre-vingt's*. It was impossible that a man could have answered that phone, Paul's phone, except himself—had he heard an echo? Not another man, not Sylvie, there was never any question of *that*. Then the other ridiculous tag line rattled through him: *the husband is always the last to know.* He felt the scissors going in.

With a hateful suspicion, and matching vision (a man's hand holding the telephone receiver, the other hand on his wife) Paul let himself be washed away on a wave of nausea. Mustn't throw up over this. Need a breath of air, or another drink—no, not a drink. He would have to think this out sitting down. When he got back to the terrace the ill-lighted deck was full of shadows and no sailors. Only Chantal and Raspoutine were there. The silence was frightening; Paul looked around for Neal.

"*Il est parti,*" said Chantal.

"*Ils sont tous partis,*" said Raspoutine.

Neal was gone, they were all gone. Paul's desolation was complete: now he would never be able to tell his brother—what?

"There's another man on my telephone," explained Paul, then translated into French, for Chantal's sake.

It was time to put away the Monopoly game. Raspoutine and Chantal helped Paul scoop the money into the canvas bag Neal had left behind. The bag reminded him of something. Paul thrust his hand into the pile of duty-free cigarettes, touched metal, and felt another cold stab in the chest. Who would ever have thought of a pistol buried under a pile of Lucky Strikes? We spread some green around and tip our hats to the ladies. Paul had no hat, so he saluted Chantal in the flip manner of the boy with the broken jaw and left two twenties on the table, for whatever.

The plane trees were full of starlings chirping in concert, screaming through Paul's brain. He stood off a moment watching the taxi driver polish his Mercedes Benz under a street lamp in front of the Société Générale—Sylvie's bank. The taxi driver had white, white hair. Paul did not remember the man's hair as white as that: maybe it was another driver, or the street lamp—or seeing Paul—had turned his hair white. The serious-looking Mercedes appealed to him. It was the kind of car you went to see your wife in. Did the driver know the village of Ys? He did. It was not until the fare was set, and Paul got in, that he realized how much the car resembled a hearse. The old man put his cleaning rag into the glove compartment and put on a chauffeur's cap. Alone in the vast passenger section, Paul wished he had sat up front with the driver.

As they drove along the empty road to Nice the driver informed Paul he had learned his scrappy G.I. English during the war. He admired Americans.

Did the antics of the American sailors in Villefranche disturb him?

"Boys shall be boys," said the driver.

They got quickly through the mustard-colored outskirts of Nice and onto the broad boulevard that led to the Côte d'Azur airport, then turned at the hippodrome into Cagnes for the road to Grasse through the *arrière pays*. The old man drove well—anyway, there was no traffic. Paul lighted a Lucky Strike and offered it to the driver, then lit one for himself.

The driver had been a Communist before the war but had become disillusioned. Now that he owned his own taxi —what was the point? He had been a practicing Catholic all his life but ceased to go to Mass after the death of his wife. But he would want to be buried in the Church, as was his wife. The French, he told Paul, did not make good Catholics. Or Communists. Priests were as venal as politicians. And a French Communist simply wanted the *voiture* of his neighbor.

This discourse seemed to have exhausted his English, for after that he spoke French.

Paul asked him if he was a father. The old man showed three fingers, then explained they were all grown now, married, and with children of their own.

"*Je suis grandpère maintenant.*"

"*Bravo.*"

The driver shrugged. There was nothing to it.

Paul had read somewhere that population was declining in France. The average French family had one and a half children. What was a half child like? Like the spectral Christine. Paul would like to have asked the old man's position on abortion. Sylvie's *intervention* had left no scars, as far as Paul knew. But a taxi was no place to discuss the right to life. It was just something Sylvie had decided to do, and Paul agreed, and she did. The hippie son of Dr. Blancheneige did it, legally, at a clinic in Vence. You needed three affidavits from doctors who had treated the pregnant woman for mental illness. Three doctors, that was easy. The operation was one of those things that should have been dramatic, but wasn't. Or was it? Paul had stayed with J-P while Sylvie drove off to the appointment in Vence. She came home three days later looking lovely, looking relieved.

Paul wanted to ask the taxi driver if he had considered the expense of a second and third child, but it was not something you discussed in a taxi. Paul and Sylvie never discussed it again. The abortion left no scars; it was, in fact, forgotten —or was it? The Swansons simply could not afford to have one and a half children, so the half child was eliminated. Or was it?

Suddenly they were in Grasse, an empty ghostly town this time of night. What time of night was it? "*Dix-heures-dix,*" the driver told him, checking his watch by the dashboard light. Paul then found his own wristwatch in his pocket, and put it on.

They stopped to urinate, both, in a *pissoir* next to Frag-
onard, where the flush was liquid waste from the *parfumerie*
—it smelled of jasmine. Then they wound upwards along
the terraced streets of Grasse to leave the city by Route
Napoleon, the road from the sea the little Corsican traveled
in pursuit of a triumphal comeback. The almost full moon
illuminated nests of pink and white chateaux tucked away
among the cypresses: somber villas of exiled Russians remembering a colder climate, the formal gardens of retired
British bank managers, or extravagant castles that could only
belong to aging *vedettes* of the Folies Bergères. Napoleon
was not the only innocent to follow his star to these parts.

By the time they had got to the village of Ys Paul had
lost heart. He knew he should not have come. The trip had
sobered him, and he did not know why he was here. Yes,
he knew. There was another man in his house, in his bed.
But what would he do—a lover there, or not—if he had to
look into Sylvie's eyes?

At first he thought of asking the driver to turn around,
but instead he suggested they both have a drink at the local
bistro.

"*D'accord.*"

The Toison d'Or was a cave with nicotine-stained walls
and no more in the way of décor than wine casks for tables
and a ceiling festooned with dangling spirals of fly paper.
The place was stifling and ill lighted, but somehow comforting. George was playing *bélote* at a back table and he
greeted Paul with a nod over his cards. His mother, in
Mother Hubbard black, sat beside the cash register, her face
covered with flies. Paul was about to order *eau de vie* but
remembered all the *eau de vie* that had flowed that night,
and thought about Nelson, after Trafalgar, shipped back to
England preserved in *eau de vie*—so he had what the driver

was having, pastis. Georges' mother poured, with trembling hands.

They wished one another *Santé*, then Paul asked the driver when he would retire.

"*Jamais*," said the old man.

"*Bravo*," said Paul.

The driver shrugged. He was a man, like Paul, who could not sleep at night. During the day he fished off the pier at Villefranche; at night he drove a taxi. The lack of sleep was nothing: there would be time for sleeping—there was the big sleep ahead.

He had bought the taxi himself, since no company would hire him—he was past the legal retirement age, and he could not be insured. One had to get around the law somehow or those *cons* in Paris would strip a man to the skin with taxes and bury him in red tape.

"*Bravo*," said Paul.

The old man lived alone.

"*Et ça marche?*" Paul asked. "Does it work?"

"*Ça marche doucement*." The driver tilted his hand from side to side to show how it works, slowly.

He was a rock, an example. It was a relief to stand in a cave with this wonder while the world came apart outside. He must stick with the old man.

"Listen. Let's go back to Villefranche."

The driver looked puzzled, but said, "*D'accord*."

But then again, on the strength of the drink, Paul decided he had come too far to turn back now.

"First, I have a commission to perform—will you wait for me here?"

"*D'accord*," said the driver. But he would be obliged to charge forty francs for every hour's waiting time. It was Paul's turn to say, "*D'accord*."

Twenty-nine

The path Paul followed was the Chemin du Paradis (which began, appropriately enough, at the cemetery), down the steep side of the rock promontory where Ys had perched since the fifteenth century. He could have found his way in the dark—he would have preferred to, in fact—but the chemin opened before him in the clear light of the huge moon that hung suspended over Ys.

He walked down past the stone wash tubs where the village women (except Sylvie, who had a Bendix) scrubbed and gossiped the morning away, past the wooden cabanon where the shepherd (another solitary like himself) lived in winter. From here on mostly olive trees clung to the narrow terraces; houses grew scarce. Behind a nearby hedge a dog whined and pulled at his chain; frogs croaked a warning in what Paul took to be French, from the stone water tanks beside the path.

Around the next turn was the view that opened out over the valley of Peymeinade, to the Esterel—which still showed the bald places burned black where a forest fire devoured the mimosa a summer ago—and to the sea. He knew the distant contours by heart, but the spectacle never failed to surprise him. On a clear morning after an all-night mistral had washed the sky you could see the faint trace of Corsica along the horizon. Cannes, at the moment, was no more than a necklace of lights far below. At this distance from the coast you could still believe in the Riviera as a background for the romantic figures out of an E. Philips Oppenheim novel. Even death was more dashing then: D. H. Lawrence coughing his life away in St. Raphael. Isadora Duncan strangling

on her own scarf on Promenade des Anglais. From the cliffside below Ys, Paul surveyed the scene from the small end
of a telescope and created the place out of an invented past
—the only way to live on in the south of France. The
Phantom Inspector, traveling only at night, could keep his
illusions intact.

Sylvie had another vision (all her visions, it seemed, were
different from Paul's): the *prana* at this height would be a
boon to J-P's respiratory system. (*Prana* was the Hindu word
for "vital air"—Sylvie had taken up the vocabulary of her
adopted philosophy.) Furthermore, she assured him, "The
price of land will surely go up to seventy francs a square
meter as soon as the tourists discover this region." It was a
truth that depressed Paul as much as it exhilerated Sylvie.

Suddenly he was standing at the foot of his own driveway,
obliged to deal with an onrush of panic, a failure of will.
He straightened himself, stood erect, swallowed, touched
his hairline and tried to think reasonable thoughts. He began
by giving thanks that Sylvie had parked the Opel under the
latticed roof of their rustic carport. She was inclined to drive
right up to the kitchen door and leave the car there, until
he warned her the relentless *Midi* sun would melt the transmission to butter. The car was the one thing Paul was more
practical about than his wife—though it was Sylvie who was
farsighted enough to keep a camera and chalk in the car,
to document collision evidence for an insurance claim
(she kept them in the glove compartment, along with the
snake-bite kit.) As he walked by the car he gave the Opel a
friendly pat on the hood, wondering, at the same time, if
that left front tire needed air.

He felt his way along the shadowed drive by touching the
cypress hedge—it had been trimmed; who trimmed it now?
surely not Sylvie—and he crushed a sprig of it between his

fingers: it smelled as always, even at night, of gin and tonic. He stepped out on the tough spongy carpet of lawn and studied the garden, his garden, won out of an indifferent soil by pure peasant stubbornness (in this he was a Frenchman in his blood and bones, this love of a southern garden), irrigated by sweat and tears. There was breeze enough to rustle the transparent paper-thin bougainvillaea leaves fallen like scraps of brittle tissue across the front of the house; he was careful not to walk there.

How dim the light seemed at the window along the balcony. When he got closer to the house he realized that a candle flame flickered behind the living room curtain. Except for birthdays, or when a mistral knocked out the electricity, Sylvie never lit candles. Paul stiffened. He analyzed the candlelight with a sudden careful sobering chill.

Would he actually do battle with a man found on the premises? (What right had Paul to these premises now? The house was not even his—the lady of the house his in name only.) The pistol he carried in the bag was a haphazard and grotesque joke. He had never fired a pistol in his life, nor would he now. What else? The vision of himself trying to separate Sylvie from her lover was a cartoon. (But the vision of Sylvie entangled with her lover made his legs go weak.) He took two deliberate steps backward—no, he would not fight.

Madame Roustan's cat came by, sneezed twice with special dignity, scratched itself on the chin with a hind paw and walked on—another night creature with *droit de passage*. There was a time when that cat would rub itself, purring, against the back of Paul's leg—but that was when he had *droit de passage* himself.

He crept across the lawn to the patio under the balcony, to listen. He heard nothing but crickets and his own troubled heart. (The creeping, the listening, was the worst of it—another measure of manhood cut from under him.) What would he say if Sylvie caught him there? "Only the Phantom Inspector, chérie. Inspecting."

Instead of climbing onto the balcony he lingered under it practicing the shallow breathing Hindu's recommended for being buried alive. He stood stiff, jarred by his own heartbeat, straining to hear what was being said inside the house. For one blind instant he pictured the Canadian in there, a ghost from the film festival, then shook himself free of that thought. If he kept this up much longer his lungs would burst, so he ventured along the side of the house to a window at living-room level.

"*J'entends quelque-chose!*"

He flattened against the stone wall. It was a child's voice—but whose? J-P's room was at the other end of the house.

"*Ce n'est rien,*" said J-P, in the reassuring tone of an older brother. Was Christine with him—or were they both hallucinations?

The voice (or voices) came from a tent set up in the garden, strung between two almond trees Paul favored for his Sunday hammock. Sylvie sometimes allowed J-P to sleep outdoors on summer nights.

The other child (if there was one) could have been any one of the outcasts of the village J-P chose as friends. He ignored the mayor's son, the doctor's daughter, and preferred instead the mazout dealer's crippled son, who hobbled about with a brace, or Hassan, the frail Tunisian (tenth of eleven children), whose nose ran without let-up, or the Jouillier girl, whose mother ran off with a trucker and left Nathalie to her grandmother and Sécurité Sociale.

"*Ce n'est rien,*" said J-P again. (He did, like his father, sometimes talk to himself.)

A flashlight came on inside the tent. Then J-P poked his head between the tent flaps, a flashlight in one hand and a bayonet in the other. By moonlight Paul could make out a crudely colored paper American flag attached to the tent pole above J-P's head. An indifferent patriot himself, Paul was touched that his son was fiercely proud of being half-American, though he had never been to the U.S. When the flashlight beam swung in his direction, Paul crouched below the window sill well out of sight, so as not to frighten him, or them. At that moment he could have snatched up the tent and fled—where?—and what to do with the extra child, if there was one and it was not Christine?

"*Ce n'est pas un loup,*" said J-P, as if calming his frightened sister. "*Le loup,*" he intoned, "*n'est pas originaire du Midi.*"

Paul repeated this talisman under his breath, in translation—"The wolf is not native to the south of France"—for he was as much in need of sustenance as his son. If the magic phrase was not completely reassuring to a child, Paul himself was vaguely comforted, and as soon as J-P's head withdrew inside the tent, he stood up.

"The wolf is not native to the south of France," he said to himself, and stared into the open window at his wife.

Sylvie's back was turned to him. She sat, not with a lover, but alone. From the position of her knees—hands resting lightly on them, thumb and forefinger touching, the other fingers delicately extended—he realized she had assumed the lotus. She was practicing *tratakam,* the gazing exercise: a candle flame flickered at eye level not far from where she sat.

The undersong of his son's voice lingered in the air. It recalled the "*Allo*" he had heard on the phone—of course, it was J-P who had answered—no solace in knowing he was a fool, for he had known that all along. Coming here had been another fool's errand in his foolish life.

Nevertheless, he had exorcised the next to last ghost: a lover. Sentiment having ruled him for so long, not even jealousy could sustain him now. If he had the power to float unseen into her perfumed aura one last time—a phantom in truth—the mock kiss he placed on the back of Sylvie's neck (where the nightdress opened, and her hair fell to one side) would have been the impulse of the fool he was: not out of love, for love had fled or floundered, but as a final taste of the faded past.

Sylvie moved gracefully into the corpse pose, which was appropriate, for she was as dead to him as he was to her.

Thirty

J-P, just out of reach, whispered to himself in his cocoon. Paul dared not approach one step closer for fear of stumbling on a tent peg. When the flashlight finally went out Paul retreated along the slope at the side of the house, noiselessly, with a careful crablike sidewise gait. He ducked under the balcony, then raced his own shadow across the moonlit patio, down the lawn between the olive trees to the carport where he leaned against the Opel's hood to catch his breath.

Paul carried his own set of car keys. When he got into the car his bulk fitted the front seat so well, his hand exactly right for the steering wheel. Only the rear-view mirror needed a millimeter's adjustment. The car started with a low hum; he did not fully slam the door until he had backed down the drive, shifted into first and was out of sight and sound of the house.

The canvas bag was beside him on the empty seat, a pistol at the bottom of it, his brother's gift. Paul could remember the look of J-P's bayonet, but he could not summon up the image of that other deadly weapon. He could, however, hear the explosion it made—the humiliating sound of an exploding cigar. To drown out the echo inside of his ear he turned on the car radio: perhaps the girl with the sexy whisper had a message for the faithful at night.

She came on in husky seductiveness, reading the news of revolution, rape, shipwreck and murder, and when she switched to the notices of missing persons Paul listened for a description of his own corporal statistics. But nobody knew he was gone. Somebody has to know you're not there before you can turn up missing.

After that came a blast of electric guitar and what passed for a love ballad among the young; impossible to turn it down, so he turned it off, for fear the wild cry might attract the notice of the highway patrol. He would hate to be stopped by a policeman and have to explain a pistol and a stolen car. The car was Sylvie's now. The pistol was a joke his brother had played on him: they had Indian-wrestled for it, and Paul won.

The dark welcome the woods offered was brooding but generous. It was easy to find the same stretch of pines where they had once been together searching for an evergreen. He parked in the very same spot. In the light of the dashboard he watched a mosquito land on his finger and begin to feed. The little things are what nibble a man to death, not the big bang.

The moon changes from one province to the next, thought Paul as he got out. (He locked the car.) A red moon raked the path ahead, and lit his way as if by neon. He followed in something of a trance.

No life here but mine, thought he, walking into the last empty place, on the threshold of the void where everything begins. A rabbit might be watching more frightened than he was. He could step on a snake, or a toad. There were birds, surely, nesting for the night.

He saw J-P's anorak bespattered by tears (as if it had rained) when Papa lost his billfold at the racetrack. A man who lost his I.D. was nobody—a cipher, whose accounts were not in order. There was still that unfinished page in his typewriter; the splendid lead soldiers still lined his mantelpiece at Roquebrune. He had never found the key to Klee.

When he came to the place he knew it by the dank smell, the mossy feel underfoot, the odor of mushroom and decay. Those were the same stones Sylvie and J-P scrambled over to escape the beast that day. Paul sat down on the damp stone and considered a cigarette, but when he fumbled in the bag for a package of Lucky Strikes his hand touched metal and he came up with the unlikely instrument.

"*Sanglier!*" he howled, one hand cupped to his mouth, the other holding a pistol. The night sounds ceased. He called out again: "Show yourself you dumb monster, I'm here!"

Paul stood up holding the pistol delicately at an oblique angle, aimed awkwardly at nothing. The point of a pistol is to point it at something, but the weapon was so unfamiliar in his hand the weight of it seemed to pull him tilted to one side.

He would speak to the thing in French.

"*Venez, venez, venez, grosse bête!*" (That was the way Madame Roustan called her cat.)

He paused, and listened, then yelled: "*Je suis là!*"

But the sly beast did not come out from behind the thorns. What did the animal want from him? A death, of course. He put down the pistol and struggled with his wedding ring. The finger was swollen from the mosquito bite, but he twisted the gold band until he pulled himself free of it, then threw it into the void. The ring disappeared so quickly in the dark he hardly sensed a release. As a souvenir it was no loss—he had a scar to remember his marriage by.

What more? Paul asked himself, waiting for a sign. He picked up the pistol—a meaningless piece of machinery now, a toy—and hurled death itself at the beast's lair behind a solid wall of thorns. He heard the weapon cut the air, saw it spinning against a piece of the moon; there was a flat thud, then it went sliding scraping through the fallen leaves. He expected it to go off from the impact (and even felt the concussion, in anticipation), but no. Nothing. It occurred to him the pistol had not been loaded.

Thirty-one

Not even the tratakam candle burned at the window: the house behind the cypress hedge was silent, the tent a dark triangle between the almond trees. He eased the gray car into its place under the trellis, and got out, somewhat shaken but nervously alive. For a moment, surveying the house, he stood in a pit of misery; then he trembled briefly like a wet dog while the night breeze cooled the perspiration on his forehead.

In the glove compartment he had found a tin box with *Fruits Confits* on the lid, a rubber band around it, containing J-P's insulin equipment. This he transferred to his brother's canvas bag. He closed the car door as quietly as possible, and locked it; then he made his way up the drive toward his son's quaint bivouac.

J-P came awake instantly, unafraid.

"Papa?"

Paul could smell his own pastis-flavored breath as he whispered, "Would you like to come with me?"

"*Oui*," said J-P, then remembered it was Papa and said, "Yes."

While J-P unzipped himself from his sleeping bag and dressed—the fringed jacket might have come from Duff's stock of Davy Crockett gear, the khaki shorts were Swiss—Paul sorted possibilities, considered borders, contemplated sanctuary. Miss Bishop would take them in, if he knew Miss Bishop. Italy was only two hours away. As for transport—would the taxi driver have waited in Ys all this time?

Never mind. Paul clapped J-P's sandals together to shake off ants. He folded the pajamas into his canvas bag: they were dry, and J-P announced, "I did not pipi."

"We'll do one together, for the road."

"Does Maman know?"

"Don't want to wake her," said Paul.

J-P left the shelter of his tent armed with a holster of sugar and a bayonet, awake and ready for whatever. At the foot of the drive father and son urinated against the hedge, projecting their twin glistening streams into the cypress, a ritual emptying.

As they passed the car Paul thought, yes, that right front tire needs air. Pursuit was inevitable; he wanted (he told himself) to be fair—he placed a gift pack of Lucky Strikes beneath the tire: the Phantom Inspector was here.

They climbed. On the steepest stretch Paul carried J-P on his back: J-P clung to his father's neck with one arm, saluting Napoleonic sentries in the dark, brandishing his bayonet at shadows. If there was no Christine (and there was not), at least the boy on his back was real.